Praise

"I nearly puked reading [Lee's] description of the corn shits." -- Vladimir Cheaver, author of I AM THE GREAT CORNHOLIO: A Philosophical Dissection of Beavis & Butthead in Dust Bowl-era Literature

"This wasn't just plain terrible, this was fancy terrible. This was terrible with raisins in it." -- Dorothy Parker, author of SUNSET GUN

"[The author's] literary skill is, of course, superior, but [the stories'] moral level is low, and their perusal cannot be anything less than harmful." -- The New York Times

"I need help reacting to something." -- Abed Nadir

GRATUITOUS FLUIDS

*a bizarro collection so depraved
the authors are ashamed to have their real
names on it*

Edited by

P. T. LeBarne-D'or and Sue D. Nimm

Featuring Stories by

S. N. Atch and S. N. Iff
Anna "The Ham Ram" Bananarama
Ben Dover, Jr.
Lavender
Brock A. Lee
H. R. Muffenstoeff
Lex Murphy
Billiam Q. Pantoprazole III
Johnny Ramrod
Sally Mustang-Leibowitz-Morgan-Jones-Washington-
Lee-Redbone, MFA, DDS
Nathan W. Taynthoemer
Klaus R. Thündercünt
Catherine Uncer Napolitano Tijeras
Helga Louise Tikkelfitz

GRATUITOUS FLUIDS

ISBN: 978-0692339152

Look, Man, I Don't Know, We Smoked a Lot of Weed
Right Before We Did This
Up Your Butt and 'Round the Corner, Uranus

"You had an arse full of farts that night, darling, and I
fucked them out of you, big fat fellows, long windy ones,
quick little merry cracks and a lot of tiny little naughty
farties
ending in a long gush from your hole."

– James Joyce, *Selected Letters*

Editor's Notes

To-Do:

– Call Dr. Kerplopzenstein about growth on testicles
    – Call Sheryl about growth on testicles after talking
    w/Dr. K.
– change oil
– call Dr. Orible RE bloody stools
– clean toilet
– call plumber
– Sharpen knifes
– Price/Buy octopus

– P. T. LeBarne-D'or

I guess C and D sharp, if I had to pick.

– Sue D. Nimm

Table of Cuntents

Great Balls of Vengeance   Page 001
    by Klaus R. Thündercünt

Cunt   Page 010
    by Lavender

Error 404   Page 011
    by Billiam Q. Pantoprazole III

Magical Rainbow Vagina   Page 022
    by Helga Louise Tikkelfitz

Cornholed by the Thunder Lizard   Page 039
    by Lex Murphy

Speed Sucking   Page 044
    by Catherine Uncer Napolitano Tijeras

Mystery Tea   Page 051
    by Anna "The Ham Ram" Bananarama

I Found Jesus   Page 057
    by Brock A. Lee

Essential Fluids   Page 064
    by Johnny Ramrod

For the Children   Page 074
     by Sally Mustang-Leibowitz-Morgan-Jones-
     Washington-Lee-Redbone, MFA, DDS

One Sexy Leafblower   Page 077
     by Ben Dover, Jr.

Moose Cleaning   Page 095
     by S.N. Atch and S.N. Iff

There's Something on the Wheel!   Page 105
     by H.R. Muffenstoeff

Barry Dingle vs. the Agents of P.O.o.P.   Page 117
     by Nathan W. Taynthoemer

Great Balls of Vengeance
an erotic *Giant Boulder of Death* fan fiction
by Klaus R. Thündercünt

So I was backpacking through the mountains and I came across this village way down in the distance of this valley and I was like, "Cool, a village," so I started towards it, figuring I could get some food and a good night's sleep or something, and as I'm walking through this farm way out on the outer outskirts, this short, stocky farmer's daughter-type comes running out of a barn at me and is all like, "Fuck my tits!" and I'm all like, "Yeah, OK," so she gets down on her knees, right there in the middle of the this fucking farm, with fences and cows and shit all around, and pulls open her blouse, her tits straight popping out, and she yanks down my pants and my dick goes hard, like, immediately, and the head smacks against her cheek but she just grabs it and shoves it between her tits and starts rubbing her massive rack up and down around my cock. She takes a second to spit down onto my johnson, 'cause, you know, friction and what not, but then she's right back to squeezing her boobs together, really getting all of my dick in there, like she's trying to bury it between her massive, sweating, heaving tits, bouncing up and down and up and down and up and down until finally I cum, all over her chin. And then she just smiles, wiping jizz from her face onto her hand and licking it off, and she's all like, "Thanks," and then totters back across the field. And I'm just standing there with my pants around my ankles and my dick swinging in the breeze, watching her disappear into the barn and wondering what in the fuck just happened.

Less than five minutes later, I've collected my shit back

up and I've cleared the farm and I'm back walking toward the village, this forest rising up on my left, and out of the middle of the fucking trees this lumberjack comes barreling out and he's all like, "Hey, bro, let me suck your dick?" and I'm not gay or anything, but I'm also not going to say no to an offer like that and I've pretty much rallied since the farm girl, so I'm like, "Yeah, OK," and he's like, "Sweet, bro," and then he drops to his knees, undoes my fly, and shoves my dick into his mouth. And, man, he goes to fucking town on me, cramming the head deep, deep into his throat and using just the right amount of teeth along the shaft, in and out, in and out, like a God damned piston, and then, bam, just like that I shoot my load and he takes off again, a beefy paw clapping my back as he races past.

So now I'm a little confused, 'cause, like, once is cool, but twice? That can't be a coincidence. I start to worry that maybe I'm dead or something, or in the Twilight Zone, but before I can figure it out, these two yeti come rolling out of the woods, all wet fur and sexy growls, until they're just fucking the shit out of each other missionary-style, the dude yeti's giant hands all over the chick yeti's massive, furry knockers, their nasty bits squishing away, right in front of me. Then this other yeti comes stomping out through these snowy pines a little ways ahead, his hand on his fuzzy cock – he was clearly jerking it to these two – but then he sees me and he's all roaring, "I'm gonna either fuck you in the ass or I'm gonna tear out your arms, your call." I kinda need my arms, and I was still literally standing there with my dick out, and the thing was moving toward me too fast to run anyway, so it wasn't much of a choice. I told him as much but the snowdude just shrugged and then he bent me over and rammed his monstrous furry dick right up my cornhole. Straight through my pants, too, I should mention. Anyway, I'm gritting my teeth, in serious pain and hoping I don't just bleed out through my ass, when, before long, he busts a nut so hard I feel a couple internal organs bruise.

He pulls out, says thanks, and goes back to watching the other two yeti going at it doggy-style, while I'm left standing there with a ruptured anus and all of my personal dignity gone.

Now, I can barely walk at this point, but I still get the holy hell out of there as fast as I can, just in case the abominable snow fucker wants to go for round two. I book it out past the forest and onto the outskirts of this sprawling-ass town that looks like it's under siege or something, with all these spike barriers lying around everywhere and a shitload of tanks driving around down in the distance. I start thinking maybe I should take my chances back in the fuck forest with the yeti, you know, 'cause at least that shit's nature and I can understand it. I'm not looking to get involved in any political or military bullshit, and I'm definitely not looking to get blown the shit up or stabbed or shot or whatever the hell else. But then, as I'm looking around at all this military hardware and tall-ass lookout towers and shit, I finally find the soldiers that are supposed to be manning it all, all of them on the ground, lying in a huge circle, each one with someone else's cock in his mouth.

I don't know what the shit's going on anymore, and I'm not about to interrupt and ask one of the military guys 'cause of the whole "not wanting to get murdered" thing, and that's when this old dude in a pair of even older underpants pops out of nowhere and asks me to give him a rimjob. I don't know why, but this was the final straw.

"What the hell is going on here?" I asked, although, to be fair, it was more of a shout and it was pretty much right in his face.

"Babaghazi rimjob yes?" replied the dude, in this high, grating voice.

3

"What? No!"

"Babaghazi rimjob please yes?"

"No, you crazy fucking crazy person!"

"Babaghazi rimjob please please? Freshly bleached anus yes?"

"What in the fuck is wrong with you? What is going on here?"

"Babaghazi rimjob you? Five dollars?"

At this point I just hit the old guy upside his head with my backpack.

"Could just said no," the old man croaked, rubbing his cheek.

"Yeah, well, that didn't seem to be working," I said. "What is the deal out here, man? Where did I hike to?"

"Don't know the boulder?" he says, his eyes all buggy.

"What the hell does a boulder have to do with all this sexing?" I ask.

So the little dude in the ratty-ass underpants explained: Turns out there's this giant fucking boulder that just shows up sometimes and wrecks up everything like it's on some bad acid or didn't get its protection money or something, so that's why the army's there, and that's why everyone's all living like it's their last day on earth all the time, trying to bone everyone and everything they can find.

Right then I didn't know if I could trust the old man in

his tattered tighty-whiteys – and really who could blame me; it's hard to take a dude seriously when you can see his withered ding dong just flopping around – so I just kinda nodded and kept walking, carefully stepping around, and then through, the neverending circle of cocksuckers, wondering why in the hell the little dude put so much stress on the "everything" part of his explanation. Really, it rattled me for some reason. I kept thinking about it as I walked toward the downtown district, every time I turned my head I was expecting to see someone humping a tree or a car or something.

I didn't really see much of anything though, not for a bit, and so I started thinking maybe it was just something in the forest, a spore or fungus or something floating in the air and making everyone sex nuts. I mean, I was several houses deep into the town at this point and not one person or abominable snowperson was even so much as giving a handjob under a blanket. I was about to write off the old man and everything else I saw/fucked as a hallucination when I literally ran into a mechanical yeti getting double-teamed by a dude and a lady. Like, I turned a corner and banged up against the robot in the middle of its three-way, all of them right there in the street, doing it in the road like that Beatle's song was a personal dare.

Anyway, they didn't seem to notice me at all, they were all a little too engrossed in each other, you know what I mean? The dude was standing in the back, absolutely going to town on some kinda exhaust port on the yeti, while the robot was bent over and using some kind of prehensile, lubricated, vibrating implement in its mouth-area to eat out the lady. She was all laying on her back, half in the street, half on the yard next to it, moaning and squirming and grabbing patches of grass from over her head, and so I stopped to watch a while, you know, for science and the spirit of discovery and what-not, and then I started jerking

5

off a while 'cause that robo-yeti was doing something to that lady that was doing something to me and, hey, when in Rome, right? I mean, I was either still tripping balls from sexy times forest, or, if Grandpa Underpants was telling the truth, just getting closer and closer to getting splattered by some kinda malevolent murder rock ever second I stayed in the valley, so, either way, I figured fuck it.

And fuck it I did.

Well, not, like, the robot or the dude or the lady – I just watched them do their thing and kept spanking it until I splooged in the gutter. I mean, after that, that's when I did fuck it. "It," in this case being, like, a dozen more farm girls with all kinds of weird fetishes and a couple random dudes and at least one sentient, consenting deer that gave me the best head of my life.

Anyway, after all that, I finally get to the village square or whatever, and I am ass-beat and pretty dehydrated so I get a sandwich and a couple sports drinks for the electrolytes, and then I just crash on a bench for a bit, fully intending to just sleep there for a few hours and then keep on truckin' through fuck valley until I end up somewhere that's actually on my map again, when I see the most attractive, gorgeous woman I've ever seen in my life. A real deal, fine-ass lady with a capital L. I mean, we're talking money and refinement just fucking dripping off of her. Skin like fine pottery, jewelry shining in the sun, a fancy dress that cost more than my college education, huge, perfect tits just about popping out of that fancy dress, an ass that could start a war. God damn everything. And I decide then and there I'm going to make it my goal while I'm here to try and bang the ever-loving shit out of her.

Turns out that wasn't very difficult. I mean, she did live in the perpetually horny and damn near predatory valley of the shadow of the death boulder after all. I didn't even have

6

to make the first move. She turned and caught me staring at her dumper, imagining all the terrible things I could do to it, and she just sashayed – and I mean fucking *sashayed*, working those hips and that skintight dress and just daring you not to ruin your pants – on over to me, leaned down so her tits were right in my eye line, and whispered in my ear, "You're going to fuck me, right now." And then she grabbed my cock, just so I definitely got the message.

In less time than it takes to explain it, she took me back to her apartment and I had her on the bed, her fancy dress on the floor somewhere beneath my dirty cargos. She's laying there, naked and spread-eagled, her perfect rack heaving, and she's moaning, calling, beckoning me towards her with one finger, the other hand rubbing up and down slowly on her shaved pussy, and she's just getting wetter and wetter, louder and louder, just waiting for me, aching for me, and my dick is like a fucking baseball bat at this point, I'm actually having trouble walking, and so she leans up and grabs my johnson and she's rubbing her wet hand up and down it and she's pulling me towards her until I'm right on top of her and so I throw her down to the bed again and she's moaning again and pulling on my cock, bringing it to her pussy, the tip rubbing up against her clit, and I thank God I came so many times earlier that day because no mortal man was gonna be able to stop himself from jizzing early in a situation like this, and even then I'm barely able to contain myself, feeling the warmth of her body against mine and listening to how hard and bad she wants it, and, oh my God, those fucking eyes, and then... then, all of a sudden, there's this rumbling.

I try to ignore but it gets worse and worse, like, knocking shit down in the room worse, so I look out the window and there is this giant, gargantuan, God damned, motherfucking, pants-shitting, city-wrecking boulder of painful, unmerciful doom just barreling down the hillside, destroying absolutely everything in its path. I mean, this shit's the size of a city block and it is just covered with spikes and *on fucking fire*. We can see it a solid mile away. We are one hundred and ten percent doomed, and that's not even bad math in this situation. Like, even a miracle would've come up short in this situation.

"Well," I say, turning to the lady, "I guess we'd better make this quick."

"Just put your cock in me already!"

And so I did. I rammed my cock all up in her and we commenced to fucking like drug-fueled rabbits on spring break getting paid to screw on camera in a country with very liberal indecency laws. It was such a God damned blur of skin and fluids and acrobatics that I'm not sure I could explain it even if I could remember it all. All of my blood was in my dick and I may have even blacked out a few times. She did things to me that made me feel things I didn't even know I could feel. I was inside every part of her with every part of me. And through it all, we both kept staring out the window, waiting for our permanent end. We just kept doing it, watching that boulder, that impending fucking doom, charging at us, and that just made us do it harder and crazier. We boned like we were asking God's forgiveness for everything we'd ever done wrong, like we were auditioning for Satan's inner circle just in case that didn't work out. We fucked the way mankind had been trying to fuck since the dawn of time. We came simultaneously, just a fucking ocean of cum everywhere, our bodies orgasming so hard and so damn intensely that we didn't even feel the boulder obliterate the apartment and tear us into stew meat.

Anyway, we're dead now. But, I mean, I was probably done anyway, right? We pretty much fucked every page out of every sex handbook and version of the Kama Sutra that ever existed, in the span of minutes, and this chick was a California dime, at least, so, you know, it's not like I was ever going to do anything better with my life. And judging by how hard her cooch clamped down on my dick when she came, I don't think she was going to either.

So, yeah. I guess if there's a point to all this, a moral or whatever, it's that whatever you do in your life, whatever lofty goals you're trying to accomplish or legacy you're trying to leave, everything you have ever done and will ever do will absolutely pale in comparison to the nasty, crazy, transcendental sex this lady and I had on that bed in that apartment in that valley on that day, so, you know, don't sweat things so much.

Cunt
by Lavender

"I am a floating, magical cunt. I can teleport. I can put out fires. I can do just about anything except get paid the same amount for doing the same amount of work as a penis. Death to all penises!"

Moments later, every man on the planet, in complete and utter pants-shitting horror, killed themselves in the incredibly real fear that women might start expecting to get what they actually deserve.

THE END, DICKS

Error 404
by Billiam Q. Pantoprazole III

"What the...?!" cried one voice in the night.

"No!" shrieked another, miles away.

"Not now!" pleaded a third, even further still.

All across the globe, men, and some women, were crying out in pent up, loin-burning frustration. Something had gone wrong. Terribly, horribly, unthinkably wrong.

***

It was a couple of minutes past eleven at night when Doug Shah's phone vibrated to life on his sparsely adorned nightstand. He reached over and blindly picked it up.

"Hello?" he asked, seven dozen frogs in his throat.

"Doug! Glad I caught you. It's Marty."

"Yeah, I know. It's a cell phone. You have your own ringtone."

"Really? What is it?"

"'I Touch Myself.'"

"The Divinyls?"

"That's the one. So, what's up?"

"We've got a big clog that needs fixing. The calls coming in just won't stop. We need you to get over there now. I've emailed you the address."

"Sure, sure. No problem. I'll be there right away."

Doug was a better than average plumber. In fact, one might go so far as to say he was the best plumber in all the land. That would require a huge survey, though, and probably a ton of paperwork. Let's just say he was damn good at what he did and leave it at that.

Doug pulled up at his destination. At least, he was pretty sure he did. The little shack he was now standing in front of resembled one of those decrepit, bombed-out hovels seen in post-apocalyptic dystopia movies, all smoke-stained, crumbling walls and a slanted tin roof, the kind of place scruffy-looking, feral children always crawled out of to make the audience go "Awwww…" and remind them of the hero's humanity right before he or she did something terrible, like rip a mutant's throat out with his hands or something.

Anyway, the professionally printed sign above the door read "The Internet." Doug thought this was an odd name for a building, and the ornamentation an odd use of overhead capital given the number of rats running around, but a job's a job. He wasn't going to turn it down. Especially at this time of night when his rates were double. He pulled out his cell and called Marty.

"Hello?"

"Marty, I'm here. I think."

"Where?"

"At 'The Internet.' It looks like the dried-up turd of an already crappy building; you sure this is the right place?"

"Excellent, yeah. That's exactly how he described it."

"He?"

"There should be someone inside to show you where the blockage is. I think he said his name was Confetti Jones."

"That's... original."

"We're all depending on you, Doug," said Marty, before immediately ending the call.

Huh, thought Doug. *That was a little odd.*

Doug, despite his misgivings, threw open what passed for the door to The Internet and walked inside. He found a man sitting behind a rickety, crumbling desk. The ornate sign on the desktop said "Confetti Jones."

"Hey!" said Mr. Jones, rising and bouncing over to the plumber.

"Hi," said Doug. "I'm here about a clog or something like that?"

"Damn right you are."

"Yeah..." replied the plumber, looking around at the basically empty shack. "I don't see a bathroom."

"Didn't you go before you got here?"

"What? No. I mean, yes." Doug furrowed his brow. "What is this place?"

"The internet."

"So... some kind of trendy hipster café? Is that why there are no tables or bathrooms or anything? And why it smells like overpriced, burnt coffee?"

"No. Is *the* internet. The actual, punctual internet. You know, the interwebs, hyperspace, online. The information superhighway with the stuff and junk and things."

"Seriously? This is *the* internet?"

"Yes."

"The one on computers?"

"That's the one."

"With all the porn?"

"Oh, you know it."

Doug looked around the single room shithole once again.

"OK... So, this clog?"

"Arabic downstairs in one of the teams in the big e."

"What?"

"Downstairs."

Doug looked at Confetti. Confetti looked at the ceiling.

"You okay?" asked Doug.

"Yeah, yeah. I'm fine justgive.org is in an egg in the market."

"Uh huh. So, maybe you can just show me the problem?"

Confetti Jones nodded, flipped his desk up on one end, and opened the trap door beneath it. He descended a steep, dark stairwell, and Doug cautiously followed his increasingly insane tour guide.

When they reached the bottom of the stairs, Confetti opened another door. Doug just stood there in shock. In front of them ran miles and miles and then even more miles of tubes of all sizes, each labeled with what they were transporting. Fantasy football, music lyrics, Star Trek erotic fan fiction, Nigerian Prince scams. It was the internet. It was all here.

"Well, better get on our way. Men everywhere are depending on you and your magic hands."

"I really don't know what... Wow!" exclaimed Doug, looking at a tube the size of the Lincoln Tunnel running just to his right. "What's in that one?"

"Miley get some penises Jessica sick as fuck for unlawful," answered Confetti.

"Excuse me?"

"Mainly tits. Some penises. More vaginas than you can shake a stick at. Butts galore. An anus or two. And a lot of fluids."

"Oh, so the porn."

"And nephews cause you never seen Barbara."

"What about my nephews?"

"No! No. Of the corner bar nothing getting through with me to go in the rain barrel Brandon mall."

"What?"

"The thing, with the stuff, that make go," the caretaker explained slowly and with obvious difficulty. "Can't go. Half-Asian blowjob stuck sticking… All the butts making all the everything slow handjob with pantyhose mature."

"OK, wait. I think I get it… That's where the clog is? In the porn tube?"

"Yes, that would be trying to tell you."

"You're not doing a very good job of it."

"Up your mother," replied Confetti. His neck twitched several times and then Doug could have sworn he became pixelated and flickered into nothing for a moment.

"This way," continued the caretaker seemingly unaware that he stopped existing for a second. "The hatch is over here and then they blow it up Lost spoilers."

Doug Shah stood in the pornography tube of the internet, up to his knees in barely-legal cocksucking. Like, literally. Just grainy piles of .gifs of MILFs and screenshots of cumshots and videos of eighteen-year-old girls with penises in their mouths and balls on their chin. The videos and what-not were manifesting themselves physically in what could best be described as a cracker-like form – comic book-thin, eight-inch by eight-inch squares akin to some kind of futuristic ultra-flat screen TVs, except without cords or edges or electronic components and running an endless loop of depravity from which there was no changing.

Doug kicked the porn crackers out of his path as he walked, tripping only occasionally as he worked his way farther and farther down the tube.

After several miles, and more German fisting pornography that he had thought humanly possible, Doug found what he was pretty sure was the clog.

"Holy motherfucking shit," he muttered.

Standing before him, filling the cavernous tunnel of porn like a sweaty, lumpy cork, was a giant of a man. At least, Doug was pretty sure it was a man. Aside from the prodigious height and girth, the creature appeared to be mostly penis and forearm. Like, eighty percent by Doug's best guesstimate – its dick had to be at least six feet long flaccid and its arms would've given Popeye pause. The man-thing's hands were as furry as a Shetland pony and its eyes were nearly empty sockets. The rest of it was malformed and sickening, just a weirdly proportioned caricature of distended fat pockets and stretches of atrophied muscles.

"Who's there?" the creature thundered.

The thing also appeared to be as blind as a replacement referee.

"Uh, me," replied Doug cautiously. "My name's Doug. I'm a plumber. I'm here to unclog the internet."

"Come closer, so I can see you better."

"No. No, I don't think I'm going to do that."

"Are you…" the creature lowered its voice menacingly, "afraid?"

"Mostly repulsed, actually."

"What're you, some kind of prude?" the man-thing taunted. "Sex is beautiful, natural. And porn is nothing but sex filmed. How can you be repulsed by the most basic of human nature?"

"It's not the porn. Well, not most of it," Doug said, remembering some of the truly batshit things he'd seen walking through the internet. "I'm talking about you, you creepy, terrifying troll."

"Troll? Troll?! Don't you understand, plumber?!" the creature roared. "I AM PORN!"

"Yeah, I really doubt anyone's spanking it to you," replied Doug. "Anyway, can you, like, move or something? So the porn can flow freely again and the internet can keep working and everyone can get back on with their lives and I can go back to sleep? I only had, like, one cup of coffee before I started this and I think it's wearing off."

The creature laughed like the Predator at the end of *Predator*, right before it blows up the jungle. It was unnerving, to say the least.

"I'd love to help you, but I'm stuck. As I mentioned earlier, I am porn incarnate and I appear to have hit critical mass. I'm wedged in here tighter than those thirty dicks in Christina Christie's vagina. Did you see that one?"

"Unfortunately, yeah, when I was walking down here. She didn't look comfortable."

"She wasn't, but she got paid well," said the manifestation of all the world's porn. "Anyway, much like the aforementioned Chris Christie in *The Governor's Gangbang XIII*, the only way to deflate me is to help me blow my wad. I've been trying to rub one out for days, but it's not happening. I swear it's never happened to me before."

"You've got to be kidding me."

"Yeah, no. I'm normally as reliable as Old Faithful. That's actually what I call my dick."

"I didn't need to –"

"Seriously, I've been trying harder than I have since I was a prepubescent teenager. Started chafing and everything. Think I might've even pulled something, no pun intended. My point is, you certainly can't fault me for trying," said the pony-handed monstrosity.

The plumber stood staring at the mountainous blob of self-gratification, a look both incredulous and terrified plastered upon his face.

"OK, look," said the porn, "if you'd rather, you could probably just build a bigger tunnel. That might work too. At the very least, it'd give me time to reload, you know?"

"Yeah, but that would take, like, I don't know, months?"

"Maybe? Like I said, this hasn't happened to me before, I'm not sure –"

"No, I meant the tunnel thing."

"Oh, that. Try *years,* plumber man. This is America, damn it. Plus we've got a Republican congress now."
Shit, thought Doug. *The giant cock is right.*

Doug Shah stood silently in the porn tunnel of the internet, thinking furiously of another option. But he knew there was only one realistic choice here: the malformed man-ball must be masturbated. People were counting on him. Balls would remain blue and pussies would remain dry if he didn't step up and choke this C.H.U.D.'s chicken. The minority of the internet that wasn't pornography was already beginning to act wonky. It was only a matter of time before the whole thing crashed, taking with it the economy and YouTube and Google and mobile streaming and Angry Birds and all the rest of society as we know it.

The country – the whole wide motherfucking *world –* was counting on Doug to spank this monstrous monkey.

"God help me."

"Yeah, I highly doubt that," said the porn. "By the way, I like my testes fondled. No need to be gentle about it, either."

***

"Oh, thank Christ," said one voice in the night.

"Oh, yeah, that's the stuff," muttered another, miles away.

"Yeah, take it, you filthy whore, take it," grunted a third, even further still.

All across the globe, men, and some women, pajamas around their ankles and hands around their naughty bits, were rocking gently and murmuring quietly so as not to wake up their significant others. The internet had been fixed. Terribly, horribly, unthinkably fixed.

Magical Rainbow Vagina
by Helga Louise Tikkelfitz

Lester Lemonthicket walked out of the bodega, a plastic bag containing a half gallon of milk and a box of marshmallow pies swinging against his knee. He stepped out from beneath the store's cloth awning, looked both ways across the street and began walking towards his apartment building.

It was at this point that Lester was stepped on by a tyrannosaurus rex.

"Son of a bitch!" the dinosaur bellowed. "I just got these sandals!"

"Told you footwear wasn't a good idea," replied his friend, a brachiosaurus.

"Can you scrape it off?" the tyrannosaur asked, lifting his foot and flailing his tiny arms.

"No. I'm not touching it. I don't know where it's been. I didn't spend millions of years asleep, surrounded by tar, just to get some human disease and die." The brachiosaur stomped a cab into scrap metal. "Why are you wearing those things anyway?"

"I wanted to blend in," said the tyrannosaur, shrugging his useless shoulders.

"And flip-flops was going to get that accomplished? How did you even get them on?"

"Fuck you, that's how."

"And I thought the stegosaurus was dumb," mumbled the brachiosaurus.

The tyrannosaurus rex leaned well into his friend's personal space, grabbed the brachiosaur by what most closely would have resembled the area where lapels would go — should the brachiosaurus ever feel compelled to wear a nice shirt — and slammed the sauropod into the side of the nearest building, spraying chunks of whatever record studios were made of everywhere.

"Don't you EVER say that about her again, you plant-eating cock monkey!"

"It's a scientific fact, man!" screamed the brachiosaurus. "Your girlfriend had a brain the size of a walnut!"

"I will bite your fucking skull clean off that ridiculous neck of yours!"

"I'd like to see you try, you pointy-toothed chucklehead."

"Chucklehead?!" shouted the tyrannosaurus rex. "CHUCKLEHEAD?!"

"You're trying to figure out if I insulted you or not, aren't you?"

"I *know* you insulted me, that was obvious, I just don't know if it warrants you becoming my lunch."

"It didn't."

"You swear?"

"I swear," said the brachiosaur. "By the way, I've actually always wanted to ask you: how did you and the stegosaur work out the, uh, physicality of things?"

"What?"

"Sorry. The boning."

"Very carefully," replied the tyrannosaurus. "You hungry?"

"I could eat. What were you in the mood for?"

The tyrannosaurus rex looked down the street full of screaming, running meat. "I think I'm pretty good right here..."

"I don't eat meat, remember?" said the salad-eating sauropod. "I need a tree or a bush or something."

"Good luck finding one in this city."

"Seriously, man." The brachiosaurus looked around. "This is some serious bullshit."

"Why don't you just try one of the humans? Think of them like tiny meat trees."

"I don't know. That's kind of a big step, buddy."

"No, THIS is a big step," said the theropod, raising his sandal-clad foot and slamming it down on several shouting

24

– and now squished – police officers. The tyrannosaurus rex held up his foot to his friend. "Go ahead, take a bite."

"That looks... unappetizing at best."

"Probably, but they're tastier smooshed. More tender."

"I don't know..."

"Do it."

"I don't really have the teeth for –"

"SMOOSHED. DO IT."

"But –"

"DO IT."

The brachiosaurus took another look around the city street, finding nothing but concrete and asphalt and metal and meat.

"I am hungry..."

"DO IT DO IT DO IT DO IT"

"OK, OK..."

The brachiosaurus craned its gargantuan neck and, gingerly snapping its teeth together, pulled most of what used to be a soccer mom free from the tyrannosaur's foot. Slowly it sucked the woman into its enormous mouth, savoring her flavor.

"You know," said the brachiosaurus, "this isn't half bad."

"You want to step on some more people? I think I see a creationist over there."

The brachiosaurus walked over to the human standing on an upturned milk crate, spewing rhetoric about there never being dinosaurs and screaming that scientists simply buried the bones and "discovered" them later to build a case against God. The sauropod leaned his massive head directly in front of the madman.

"Hey, buddy."

The protester glared at the dinosaur for a moment and then said, "Still doesn't prove anything! If I don't see it on Fox News it doesn't exit!"

"Squish!" shouted the brachiosaur.

"What?"

"No," interrupted the t-rex, "you can't just say 'squish,' you have to actually step on them."

"Oh, right." The brachiosaurus raised his gigantic foot and brought it down on top of the creationist, the guy standing next to him, and three cars.

Squish!

Crunch!

"There you go," said the tyrannosaurus. "I think you're getting the hang of this."

"That was fun."

"Told you. Want to keep squishing?"

26

"Let's find a park with a lot of kids!"

***

When the dinosaurs arrived at the park they made a startling discovery: the park was holding its annual Dinosaur Adventure Fun Time celebration. Littered throughout the acres of grass were plastic, life-size replications of all sorts of extinct creatures.

"What the fuck is this?" asked the horrified brachiosaurus.

"They're all frozen!" answered the tyrannosaurus rex. "We've got to set them free... and then build an army to overtake the humans! They've developed some kind of freeze ray!"

"Uh..." moaned a muffled, near death, voice.

"Did you hear something?" questioned the t-rex.

"I think so. Lift up your foot."

A tiny teenage girl was twitching slightly against the dinosaur's sandals. She was convulsing and bleeding, but she was still alive. Technically. The majority of her body had been crushed by the colossal foot, but her head was wedged between the grooves of the gargantuan footwear.

"Oh my God," said the brachiosaurus, "it's still moving! Stomp it harder!"

The tyrannosaurus did as instructed and slammed the girl into the ground repeatedly.

"Is it... Is it dead?"

"I… I think so…"

"Man, what the FUCK did you do that for?!" asked Kurt Vandersnootch, a white, dread-locked, teenage male, banging his tiny fists against the tyrannosaur's foot.

The brachiosaurus craned his exceedingly long neck down to the ground and stared at the man, eye to eye.

"Why are you doing that?" it asked. "How could that possibly be a good idea?"

"Tina was my girlfriend, you assholes! And I take a lot of multivitamins," said Kurt. "I'm not afraid of you! I could do this all day."

"You do know," warned the brachiosaur, "that he'll eventually have to pee."

"I don't – Oh. That sounds all kinds of unpleasant."

The tyrannosaurus nodded its humongous head. It didn't feel the need to inform its new human friend that it had already taken care of that, and instead took this as an opportunity to not seem like a wimp, a common shame for most tyrannosaurus rexes.

"So, uh, dinosaurs, huh?" asked Kurt. "How's that working out for you?"

"Not bad," said the brachiosaur.

"Lonely," moaned the tyrannosaurus.

"What's wrong with him?" asked the teenager, pointing a thumb at the t-rex.

"He misses his dumb girlfriend."

"Shut up! She wasn't dumb!" shouted the carnivore. "She was a stegosaurus. She was perfectly smart... for what she was."

"See," said the brachiosaur.

"I do," said Kurt, turning his attention to the now-sobbing t-rex. "At least you can take comfort in the knowledge that since her brain was so small she probably didn't know she was dying."

"She's not dead."

"What now?"

"She's not dead. She got bitten by a zombie pterodactyl and ran off – well, shuffled off, technically – and got stuck in a tar pit somewhere."

"That still sounds pretty dead to me."

"That's because you're an idiot human," said the brachiosaur. "We got stuck in another tar pit a short while later. That stuff preserved our asses right up until last week when some oil company drained the pit."

"But tar isn't the same thing as oil..." replied Kurt.

"I never said the oil company was smart."

"True."

"Anyway, they siphoned all the tar, we woke up, my t-rex friend here made a quick meal out of them, and then we stomped off into the sunset."

"Becky loved sunsets," sniffled the tyrannosaurus.

"They are pretty," added Kurt.

"I think sunrises are better," retorted the brachiosaur.

The tyrannosaurus rex tried to slap his formerly extinct companion, but missed – by, like, thirty feet.

"I almost felt a breeze," taunted the vegetarian.

"Well, tell me if you feel this."

The tyrannosaurus rex lunged forward and clamped his teeth down on the brachiosaur's neck, biting clean through. The brachiosaur's head fell to the ground, yelling for as long as it could.

"You motherfuck–"

"Dude," said Kurt. "That was... I don't..."

"I take my sunsets very seriously," said the t-rex.

"Good to know. Anything else I should be aware of? How do you feel about rainbows?"

"Hmm..." mumbled the tyrannosaurus. "How do you feel about them?"

Kurt felt a lump grow in his throat.

"Fuck... 'em...?"

The dinosaur bent down to be eye-to-eye with its new human friend.

"Sounds good to me. How would you go about doing that?"

"Huh?"

"Fucking a rainbow. Your suggestion intrigues me. Plus I think it'll help me get over Becky."

"But just a few minutes ago you were all set to dig her out of the tar and stuff."

"Yeah, but that seems like a lot of work. Plus I don't think millions-year-old stegosaurus pussy could compare with a magical rainbow vagina."

"Where are you even getting that from?"

"What? Why wouldn't rainbows have vaginas? Everything has vaginas."

"I don't mean to get your hopes up, but…"

"But what?" snarled the tyrannosaurus, leaning down and flashing his gigantic, bloody teeth dangerously close to the human.

"But there's, uh, only *one* magical rainbow vagina in existence. On the planet. Near Alaska. And it's guarded by a squad of hippopotamus ninjas. Among other things."

"I'm a dinosaur. I could take a hundred hippos."

"I don't think you understand just how large and angry these hippos are."

"Take me to the vagina NOW or I will eat you."

"Fine. I'll take you, but you think I can ride on your head or something? I don't feel all that safe with your whale-sized feet stomping so close to me."

"I suppose that would be fine."

"Great! Although I will need to build some kind of chair for up there; it doesn't look that comfortable."

"Good point. I don't want your butt on my head."

***

Kurt Vandersnootch, having duct-taped a chair cushion to the tyrannosaur's head, rode his dinosaur friend across the country, all the way to the wide open plains of Seattle.

"Crap," said Kurt, "it's raining. Should've added an umbrella."

"You ain't sticking anything else on my head, buddy."

"Fine, fine."

"Are we getting close?"

"I don't know. You had the map."

"Was that the only one?"

"Yeah. Why? What did you do with it?"

"Nothing."

"Why do I doubt that?"

"You're a very suspicious person, aren't you?."

"Or maybe it's because you did something stupid?"

"I don't know what you're talking about. It's not like I wrapped someone in it like a burrito and ate them."

"It's not?"

"Okay, maybe it is."

"Why? And how? Your arms are so... puny."

"Fuck you, that's how."

"I'm more offended that you didn't think to offer some to your new friend."

"You eat people too?"

"Well... I never considered it, but I also never thought I'd be riding a dinosaur either, so I suppose my preconceived notions of acceptable behaviors in society are a little skewed at the moment."

"Huh?"

"I'm willing to try anything once."

"Well, I kind of wolfed it down, but it feels like there's still something stuck between my teeth. If you're desperate."

Kurt's stomach rumbled loudly. "I guess I am."

The teenager climbed down the tyrannosaur's head and into its mouth. He inched his way along the dinosaur's lip to the offending chunk of people and map. Carefully, he plucked the burrito remnants from between the dinosaur's teeth.

"Jesus, this is enough for, like, three people."

"What are you implying?"

"Nothing, nothing. I'm just saying, that's a lot of food."

"I'm a dinosaur, damn it! For my height and age, my weight is very attractive!"

"I know, I wasn't saying that!"

"Saying what?"

"Anything, I wasn't saying anything!"

"Damn right," said the t-rex. "Now get the hell off of my lip, you taste delicious."

"On it."

Kurt scrambled back up the tyrannosaur's head, people burrito in hand. He situated himself on his cushion and… just sat there.

"Well, what are you waiting for?" asked the t-rex.

"This is a big step for me, man!"

"I got the herbivore to eat some."

"Are you taunting me?"

"Yes."

"That won't work. I need to do this on my time."

"DO IT DO IT DO IT DO IT"

"Jesus, you're annoying."

"DO IT DO IT DO IT DO IT"

"OK, fine."

Kurt took a bite of the other people (that most likely contained his recently deceased girlfriend) and chewed it slowly. He chewed it some more and finally swallowed with a forceful gulp. Then he threw up over the side of the tyrannosaurus rex.

"Dude!" yelled the mammoth beast. "You got that all over me. The hell, guy?"

"Sorry," said Kurt, continuing to vomit on his dino buddy.

"What was that?" snarled the beast.

"Nothing. Don't worry about it."

"No, it was something. What was that?"

"I may have puked on your head."

"You asshole." The dinosaur shook its head violently in an effort to remove as much of the sick as possible. In doing so, Kurt was thrown a couple hundred yards. Into the side of a building. Made out of stone. Really hard stone. Kurt died immediately. One might even say he exploded from the impact.

"Is it gone?" asked the tyrannosaurus.

Kurt obviously did not answer.

"I'm going to take your silence as a 'no.'"

The tyrannosaur approached the blood-stained wall and tilted its head slightly.

"Pal?"

Silence.

The tyrannosaur shrugged.

"No sense letting him go to waste."

The tyrannosaur licked what was left of Kurt from the wall with tremendous satisfaction.

***

The tyrannosaurus rex, only vaguely aware of which way he was going and what he was looking for but desperately craving an Eskimo Pie for dessert, made its way to the northernmost parts of Canada. It was a long trip, and there were a lot less Canadians now, but the t-rex really liked the taste of Inuit.

The dinosaur trudged over a rather large snow bank only to discover a strange furry creature standing alone in the middle of nothing but endless miles of snow, directing nonexistent traffic. Slowly, the tyrannosaurus made its way toward the large fluffy monster. The yeti took notice.

"A horsie!" screamed Carol, the yeti, and galloped toward the dinosaur, its intention very clearly being to ride the tyrannosaurus rex.

"Oh, crap."

The tyrannosaurus rex made a break for it. If there was anything that dinosaurs hated, it was yetis who mistook them for horses. One would think it was not a common occurrence, but one would be very, very wrong.

"Horsie, slow down!" cried Carol, bounding after the carnivore.

"Crap, crap, crap."

Fighting against the snow, the t-rex stumbled up and over another large snow bank. It began running down the far side, only to realize there was no far side. The snow bank had simply ended with a sheer vertical drop.

"CRAP CRAP CRAP"

The tyrannosaurus flailed its tiny arms impotently.

Carol, looking down from the edge of the snow bank, said, "Stupid horsie. Horsies can't fly." Then she walked back to her imaginary intersection and started cleaning up the invisible thirty-seven car pile-up that ensued in her absence.

***

The tyrannosaurus remained broken and motionless in the snow. It slowly opened its eye, the one that hadn't burst upon impact with nearly a mile of compressed snow.

"Damn yeti," it mumbled.

It started to get up – a daunting task with those tiny arms, even without the massive physical trauma – and noticed something colorful off in the distance.

"I found it," it gasped. "I can't believe I found it."

As the blood from its enormous cranial hemorrhage stained the snow, the dinosaur stared in awe at the gaping genitalia glowing on the horizon. Slowly, the t-rex dragged itself toward the magic rainbow vagina.

"Just... a few... more... thousand... feet..."

Sadly, the dinosaur's ridiculous arms and shattered skeleton made the task nearly impossible to accomplish in a timely manner. The tyrannosaurus only made it thirty feet before a massive ice storm swept in from the north.

"No!" it shouted. "Nooooooo–"

The dinosaur was flash frozen mid-scream. The tyrannosaurs rex used the last few moments before it lost consciousness to curse its tiny arms and shed a single tear for the magic rainbow vagina.

"Forever shall it remain unhumped," thought the dinosaur.

Then a ninja hippo appeared and squatted over the t-rex's prostrate head, directly above his working eye.

"Oh, dear God, no. No! Not –"

The very last thing the tyrannosaurus ever saw was a hippopotamus taking a crap on its head.

Cornholed by the Thunder Lizard,
or:
Stego-sore-ass
by Lex Murphy

... and then the dinosaur rammed its turgid member into the woman's butthole, over and over again, Christie typed, moaning softly in her leather desk chair. *Over and over and over again, plowing Urga the way all cavewomen wanted to be plowed.*

The author slid one hand into her damp, purple underwear and continued writing with the other.

The stegosaurid's cock stretched Urga's ass in an erotic way. Christie began moaning louder. *"Fuck me, stegosaurus!" Urga grunted, "Fu;/klllllll*

The college student involuntarily clenched her free hand, nearly breaking her keyboard. She worked her clitoris, faster and faster, fantasizing about being raped by dinosaurs. She stifled a scream.

From the other side of the dorm room, Christie's roommate, Gretchen, grumbled. The coed's eyes fluttered open.

"What are you doing?" she asked.

"Who, me?" Christie replied, pulling her hand from her underwear and wiping her fingers on her t-shirt. "Uh, nothing."

"You're writing more dinosaur erotica, aren't you?"

"No."

"I can see it on your screen."

"People are buying it!"

"Yeah, ironically."

"Well, I'm writing it ironically."

"Then why was your hand in your panties?"

"I get really turned on by making money."

"And what are you going to do with all this money?"

"Buy a disguise and a fake ID and go back to the Natural History Museum."

"Why would you need a fake –"

"Because they banned me."

"For…?"

"Fellating all the dinosaur skeletons."

"You have a problem, Christie."

"No I don't."

"Really?" asked Gretchen. "What are you going to do when you get to the museum this time?"

"Fuck all the dinosaur skeletons."

"That's the definition of a problem."

"I swear, it's not! My therapist said so!"

"That homeless guy who hangs out in the quad is not a therapist!"

"He used to be!"

Gretchen sighed. "Christie," she began, "I have a very real question for you: If I were to hand you a magic amulet that could take you back to dinosaur times, would you want it?"

"I would grab that amulet in a heartbeat. I would murder you six times for it."

"And once you had it, you would…?"

"Fellate all the real dinosaurs, for reals."

"You know that would never work, right?"

"What, a time travelling amulet? I know that."

"No, I have one of those. I meant the dinosaur fellating."

"Bullshit!" cried Christie, visibly angry. "I could totally suck a dino dick."

"Twenty bucks says you're wrong."

"Go get the amulet, bitch. And your video camera."

Gretchen threw off the comforter and walked to her closet. Squatting down, her sleeping thong nearly lost in her

41

apple-bottomed ass, the coed rummaged through an old canvas duffel bag, finally emerging with the magic amulet.

"Come here," she ordered, holding the talisman with two hands. "Grab the other side."

Christie did as instructed, her hands – among other things – trembling with anticipation. Gretchen said the incantation and, in a very pink puff of smoke, the roommates were transported back to the Jurassic Period.

"Holy shit!" said the dinosaur erotica writer, her vagina becoming noticeably more moist through her dripping underwear. "This is fucking awesome! I'm gonna blow every one of these dinosaurs!" Christie turned and pointed at an enormous stegosaurus grazing nearby. "Starting with that one!"

The coed ran towards the creature, screaming, "Put your giant cock in me!"

The stegosaurus, startled, turned to flee, swinging its massive spiked tail wildly behind it. The tail caught Christie squarely in her midsection, the impact squishing her organs like a thousand baseball bats, the spikes tearing through her like a fork through wet tissue. The dinosaur erotica writer's corpse rained to the ground in several dozen pulpy pieces.

"Looks like you owe me twenty bucks, you stupid twat!" shouted Gretchen.

Holding the amulet in both hands again, she began the incantation to return home, only to be interrupted by several large teeth tearing into her flesh. The college student was quickly devoured by an allosaurus BECAUSE DINOSAURS ARE TERRIBLE, HORRIBLE MONSTERS WHO WILL EAT YOU AND YOUR

LOVED ONES WITHOUT A SECOND THOUGHT AND IF YOU'RE FANTASIZING ABOUT FUCKING THEM YOU'RE BRAIN-DAMAGED AND I HATE YOU OH MY FUCKING JESUS I HOPE YOU DIE YOU STUPID CUNT HOW ARE YOU ACTUALLY SELLING BOOKS GO TO HELL AND ROT YOU STUPID UNTALENTED HACK

THE END

Speed Sucking
by Catherine Uncer Napolitano Tijeras

She leaned back in her chair as her new date slowly stood up in front of her and began undoing his trousers. He deliberately slid his zipper down and let his pants fall to the floor. What about the belt, you ask? One does not wear a belt when one goes speed dating.

He stood in front of her, boxer-briefs at eye level, as she slowly licked and parted her lips. Her hands shot from her lap, where she had already been three knuckles deep, and dove down his underwear like Dwayne Wade doing something unspeakable with a basketball. She pulled his erect love muscle out and began jerking him off like a champ. She oozed out of her chair and walked over to him all the while still on her knees. And also never letting go of the cock. You never let go of the cock.

Having just arrived at her destination – Penis Town – she settled in and popped that longshoreman right in her upstairs wang holster. He tasted okay, she thought.

"Mmm," she mumbled, his sticky wicket pressing against the back of her throat.

That was the stroke that ejaculated the camel's doodle.

She swallowed and with a wipe of her mouth she said, "Next."

***

44

Tired of the same old guys you meet in Speed Dating? Why not try Speed Sucking? What is Speed Sucking, you ask? Allow us to explain!

Ever bring a man home after an incredibly amazing date only to have the entire night ruined due to your new friend's disappointing penis? At Speed Sucking we know how important good dick is to you ladies. That's why we think it's vital that you know what he's packing before he starts packing it in you. Not convinced? Here's what some satisfied customers said about our service!

Sam from Toronto: "I was on the fence about this one guy and then I saw his junk. Now we're engaged! Thanks, Speed Sucking!"

Heather from Portland: "Things were going great. We had a lot in common, both wanted kids and he didn't live with his mom. Then he came on my face. Which was fine, I guess, it's just... it tasted like cat feces. I'm glad I found that out early, though, before – What? What do you mean, 'How would you know what cat shit tastes like?' You don't? Why are you looking at me like that? Hey, come back! I still have more to tell!"

Cody from Trenton: "Fuck you guys! Now I can't give these bitches my gonorrhea. Guess I'll just go die alone in a ditch somewhere. Trenton!"

As you can clearly see, the service we provide is the cock of the walk. So cum see us today. And we'll see you next Tuesday.

Cumming later this year, Gay Speed Sucking. Watch out, Grindr.

***

She leaned back against her chair, waiting for the next penis to present itself and started rubbing her supple nipples through her shirt. She brought her thumb and index finger up to her waiting mouth and licked them. Licked them something sloppy.

Her now moist hand made its way passed the buttons on her blouse and pinched her left nipple.

"Oh fuck," she whispered.

She continued squeezing her perky flesh as her other hand made its way towards her lady garden. Her panties, as well as the chair, were soaked. Not to mention her skirt, which was also drenched, but on the floor, below the moist chair, in a puddle. A clear puddle... That was slowly becoming redder and redder.

"Oh fuck fuck fuck," she screamed both in realization that she had just gotten her period and that she was about to cum like a superfreak.

"Hi, I'm Jeff. I'm here to show you my penis," said her new suitor, completely disrupting her flow. Just the one flow, though. Her Aunt Flow was still going strong. As her panties, chair, skirt and floor could certainly attest to.

"Not now, Jeff."

Not knowing what to do next, and less than a little weirded out by the pool of blood beginning to encircle the two of them, Jeff dropped his pants and began furiously whacking off.

"The fuck do you think you're doing?" she asked. "I said good day, sir. Get that shriveled-up little acorn dick out of my sight."

46

"Come on, baby," said Jeff, slapping his minnow. "You know you like this."

She grabbed a cloth napkin off the table beside her, rubbed it around the canyon inside her, pulled it out, grabbed the currently being masturbated penis in front of her and pulled Jeff to his knees.

"Oh, the rough stuff, eh? Now you're speaking my language, cutie."

"Enough with the nicknames, you used tampon."

"I like it when you talk dir–"

She grabbed Jeff's actual head, finally within arms' reach, and shoved his nose deep within her Sex-Box One. Then she queefed like she never queefed before.

It just so happened that she was having an extra heavy uterine shedding.

***

You thought Speed Sucking was already perfect? You thought there was nowhere else we could go now that the gays are on board? Well, you thought wrong, motherflubbers! Introducing Extreme Speed Sucking! Everyone's blindfolded! And there's no talking allowed. Blind sucking, people! Straights, gays, men, women and the occasional wildebeest. That's right! Wildebeest!

EXTREME SPEED SUCKING! RIDE THE BEEST!

***

Having picked up where she left off before she was so rudely interrupted by Jeff – currently passed out on the floor – she was finally close again. Her blood- and cum-streaked legs shook with such intensity it was like they were trying to quiet the world's most annoying baby.

"Oh fuck, I'm cumming!" she screamed through the TGI Fridays.

The waves of exhaustive pleasure rolled over her, relaxing every inch of her. A slight rumble erupted from her stomach.

"Hi," said her next suitor. "I'm Lincoln. I like to call my penis The Great Emancipator."

"Well, hello," she said towards Lincoln's crotch.

"You like that? Then check this out!"

Lincoln tensed up for a good minute and then his gargantuan leviathan shot his clothes straight off his body, causing his potential bedroom buddy to orgasm all over again.

"Wow," she said breathlessly, "I think I just shit myself."

And in fact, she had. With such force and veracity that it blew a hole through the chair and landed right on her skirt. Due north of Blood Lake.

"Fuck me," said Lincoln. "Right here. Right now. In your expired eggs and shit. With this behemoth of a strap-on." He produced the strap-on from his anus.

"Sold!"

Jambo, everyone! By now I'm sure you've all had the pleasure of experiencing your own Speed Sucking suckcess story. Let's run down the list before we go and announce something new. That's for later.

Speed Sucking: Millions Satisfied.

Gay Speed Sucking: Millions Satisfied.

The Original Extreme Speed Sucking: Horrific Idea. Our Bad.

The NEW Extreme Speed Sucking (100% Less Wildebeest): Millions Satisfied. At Once!

Wildebeest Speed Sucking: One Really Weird Guy Satisfied.

Don't worry, my lesbian sisters, we haven't forgotten you. That's why this fall we are introducing Lesbian Speed Sucking! When her lips get split, suck that clit!

***

"Fuck!"

"Fuck!"

"Oh, fuck! Fuck! Fuck!

"Right there! Fuck me!

"Yeah! Yeah! Take it!

"Cum in me! I need it!"

"Fuck!"

"Fuck! I'm going to cum!"

"Me too. DO ME!

They came together, still at the Manhattan Boulevard TGI Fridays just outside of New Orleans on August 23rd, 2005. Nearly two-thousand people died and over a million were displaced due to the ensuing flood. The region was never the same again. Some say it was all due some crazy natural disaster or some outlandish thing that could only happen in some fucked up collection of bizarro authors. But we know what really happened.

A shitload of cum.

Mystery Tea
by Anna "The Ham Ram" Bananarama

"So... what is it?"

"Dunno. Found it in the back."

"Why would I drink it then?"

"Half price?"

"Still not doing it for me."

"Could give you superpowers."

"It could just as likely give me cancer."

"Eighty-five percent off."

"Ninety?"

"That's basically stealing."

"Eighty-seven?"

"OK, fine," sighed Lori Slanderson, "but I'll barely make a profit off this."

"Isn't it all profit?" scoffed Michelle Buttafucco. "I thought you 'found this in the back.'"

"Shut up," said the barista, adding *you stupid cunt* in her

51

head. "Do you want it or not?"

"Yeah, I guess so," replied the customer, with the addition of *you fucking bitch* mentally. "Give it to me."

Oh, I'll give it to you, slut.

I hope you fucking die.

You cum-gargling whore.

You coupon-accepting daylight prostitute.

Two-cent skank.

Classless harlot.

"Coming right up!" said the barista with a smile.

"Wonderful! Thank you!" replied Michelle, equally as smiley.

Lori Slanderson turned to the back counter and started on the mysterious brew. As the water boiled she loaded up the cup with almost everything the small coffee shop had to offer.

"A pinch of sugar, a spritz of lemon, some ground nutmeg, more than enough chocolate syrup..." she whispered under her breath, assuring that this tea packed a punch.

The kettle blared its unholy demon-wail signaling that time had drawn near. Lori poured the bubbling water into the cup. It mixed with what seemed like all of God's creation as the tea bag bounced its way to the surface.

She called back to her friend at the counter, "Milk?"

"Yes, please," answered an eager Michelle.

"All right!"

Lori bent down and pulled out a small glass container from the mini fridge under the counter. She poured what looked to be the thickest dairy creamer in the world into the tea.

"Should I leave the tea bag in?"

"Yeah, I like to steep that shit."

I bet you do, thought Lori as she carried the cup over to her customer, *you clown-fucking, monkey-sucking super-bitch.*

I bet you raped your dog, thought Michelle.

Lori placed the cup on the counter in front of her friend.

"Actually doesn't smell half bad," commented Michelle, holding her blonde hair to one side as she leaned over to inhale the distinct aroma of whatever the hell was inside that cup.

"Oops!" said Lori, suddenly realizing that there was one more step that could be taken. "I forgot to stir it."

She reached under the counter, stuck her hand into the trash bin and pulled out a used plastic tampon applicator. She dunked the dual-colored tube into the tea and began to stir.

"What the hell is that?" cried Michelle, pointing at the

red and white feminine hygiene product mixing up all the goodness that lay in wait for her mouth.

"Oh, this?" said Lori, thinking extraordinarily fast. "These are our new flavor blast stirrers. I know it *looks* like a tampon and all, but that's just where we got the idea from. The larger end of the tube holds the mixture and then we just press down on this plunger up here and it injects your tea or coffee with a refreshing burst of flavor."

"Oh. That actually sounds… exactly like something a coffee place would do."

"We thought so. That'll be, fuck, I don't know, fifty cents?

"OK. Deal."

Michelle Buttafucco dropped two quarters on the counter and then brought the cup up close to her lips. It was only then that she noticed a sadistic grin beginning to show itself on Lori's face.

"Maybe you should have the first sip," she said slowly, putting the cup back on the counter and smiling grandly. "After all that hard work you put into making it, it's only fair that you reap the benefits before me."

"You're so sweet, Michelle, but I couldn't," replied Lori, smiling like a fucking lottery winner. "This is embarrassing, but I'm in the middle of a crazy herpes outbreak on my lower lip so I wouldn't want to contaminate your beverage."

"Sweet sexually transmitted Jesus! That's awful, Lori. I'm so sorry to hear about that."

Sure you are, you toxic, brotherfucking cunthole, thought Lori.

Michelle pressed the ceramic mug against her lips and the chunky liquid flowed into her waiting mouth. Her tongue was assaulted by what seemed like dozens of familiar flavors, but it wasn't until the congealed glob of semen slipped in and slapped her in the uvula that she realized her tea might not be entirely on the level. She swallowed in horror, but also a little bit out of habit.

"The fuck did you just give me?"

"Oh, lots of things," chirped Lori, absentmindedly running her fingers across the counter, "but mainly two-month-old splooge and a tea bag full of a homeless man's crab-infested pubic hair. All mixed together with my used tampon applicator."

Michelle immediately vomited all over the coffee shop floor. Clearly visible in the pile of puke were several dozen little, wrinkled hairs, all clearly standing at attention.

"Why would you do that," Michelle spat, in between dry-heaves, "you sadistic, goose-fucking, Hitler-fingering harpy?!"

"You slept with my fucking boyfriend, you fucking nut-slapping slut! Not to mention the herpes he got from your disease-riddled cunt. Which I now have, thanks to you."

"You're the cunt," countered an increasingly dehydrated Michelle, "you cunty cunt. If you'd let him go around back then maybe he wouldn't need to get it from me."

"You shit-headed, canyon-crotched bitch! I've got a motherfucking welcome mat at my back door! And I guarantee you, ten-to-one, it's tighter and better toned than any stank, stretched-out orifice you bring to the bedroom. "

"Not what I heard, Ms. Vaginal Flappiness 2014." Michelle finally got around to slamming the mug onto the counter, spilling boiling pube water onto Lori's apron. "Well, to be fair, I really couldn't hear that much while I was sucking his di–"

The barista slammed a wire rack of tea bags against Michelle's chin. Then she lunged over the counter, tackling her customer and driving her to the ground, her knees on Michelle's flat chest. Then, finally, Lori stood, grabbed the cash register and smashed that cock-gobbling, no-titted, Walmart-wearing skank bitch's God damned motherfucking slut head in.

And there the barista stood for a solid five minutes, her chest heaving, damn near foaming at the mouth, over the now-headless corpse of that fucking whore, Michelle. The ever expanding pool of blood began to soak into Lori's shoes.

All around her, dozens of hipsters and people who didn't know a damn thing about good coffee stared in horror.

"She didn't tip me," said Lori.

It was her most profitable day at the coffee shop ever.

I Found Jesus
by Brock A. Lee

Rachel Bunn's butthole was receiving the pounding of its life as her gaze tried to remain focused on the interracial midget porn playing on the couple's sixty-inch television. Harry Bunn knelt on the bed behind her ramming his pork sword deep inside her poop shoot. Simultaneously, Rachel was also being penetrated by a green dildo the size of The Hulk's forearm, but twice as veiny.

Her husband picked up the pace which caused her to orgasm violently. Her pussy clenched so tightly that it forced the superhero's arm out of its hidey hole. The green fist bounced off the bed and then up, nailing Harry in the bean bag. He quickly withdrew his tube steak out of her gaping refuse hole only to be trailed by what one would guess to be last night's dinner. The chunks of corn were a dead giveaway.

"Jesus Christ," she said, quite visibly winded. "I haven't cum like that since I was doing charity work for that inner city Cocks for Glocks program. So many black guys!"

"Uh, a little help?" said Harry, still covered in shit and vaginal juice. "Would you be a doll and grab me a towel?"

She looked back at him. Several dozen kernels of corn were slowly sliding their way down his face and chest, leaving brown streaks behind. She burst out laughing immediately. A good minute later she said, "I don't think my legs work."

"Please? I really don't want to drip any of this on the carpet."

She sighed and tried to get up. Her legs actually couldn't move.

"Hmm," she began, "honey, I think you might have really paralyzed me."

"Bull," said Harry, slapping her leg hard. Not really hard, but hard enough.

"Nothing."

"Weird," he said creepily staring at the TV.

"Ya think?"

Harry raised a finger and said, "Shh…"

"You cripple me and you tell me to be quiet just so you can watch some well-endowed midget drill a Rihanna look-a-like?"

"No! Well, yes, but look! That little guy looks like Jesus."

"Huh," said Rachel, "he really does."

Harry laughed, "He's so deep in that bitch that he's about to disappear…" Harry trailed off.

"What's wrong?" asked his recently gimped wife.

"I think I have an idea for my next book."

"All right," said Robert January, editor-in-chief at Kids First! Publishing, "but I don't see how you giving your wife the best sex of her life really applies to a book pitch."

"I'm just setting the scene, Bob."

"Fine. I just have one question. No, two questions."

"Sure."

"Do you plan on including this little preface in the book?"

"No. Some things should be kept quiet."

"I see. Good. And how's your wife? Can she walk yet?"

"Nope," replied Harry with a smile.

"Impressive."

"Thanks."

"So, your book idea?"

"Right. You know those books where you have to find that guy in the striped shirt and shit? There's all sorts of other people around and things and stuff."

"Great pitch. And yes."

"Cool, so instead of that normal guy we use Jesus Christ. And instead of waving or standing there like an idiot we have him sodomizing an altar boy. From behind. With both of them looking at the reader and giving a double thumbs-up."

"I don–"

"Oh!" remembered Harry. "On the kid's ass, Jesus will have a bowl of something. One page it'll be cereal. Next oatmeal. Maybe an extra thick vat of sour cream."

"Are you high, Harry?"

"No, why?"

"Well, where should I begin? How about that you started off by telling me about an extreme night of love-making with your wife in which you paralyzed her from the waist down. Follow that up with your new book idea. You know we publish books for kids, right? I don't think a book that has Jesus butt-fucking his way through the line at a Taylor Swift concert is really going to sell."

"That could be one of the scenes! Would have to be boys though."

"You're telling me Jesus doesn't care for poontang?"

"Well if the popes are any indication…"

"Stop. No. We're not doing it. Father McGooch is on our Board of Directors. I don't think he'd be all that supportive of this."

"Something tells me he might," suggested Harry suggestively.

***

Robert January and Harry Bunn entered Father Giuseppe McGooch's office and told him the idea. To only one of their surprises, the preacher loved it. So much so that he began fondling himself under his robes.

"I'd like to pre-order five," he said, his breathing growing more rapid.

"Five!" exclaimed Robert. "But why?"

"He clearly likes the idea and wants to support it," suggested Harry.

"Well, that," said Father McGooch, "and they'll probably get soiled so I'll need a couple as back-ups."

"Hm," said the two men opposite the man of God.

"I just have one suggestion," said the priest. "Instead of it being a cartoon like the original, how about I just dress up as Jesus and go out and pop some anal cherries in public."

"With the expressed written consent of their parents?" added Harry.

"Of course," said Father McGooch with a wink in Robert's direction.

"Well, I like this idea even more," said Harry. "Let's spread the word of God with this man's holy phallus... I mean chalice."

"What on Earth has come over you two?!" exclaimed Robert. "This is supposed to be a publisher for kids! Not a publisher that promotes violating kids! You guys are sick. I quit. Get someone else to run your child butt-sex factory."

"OK, sure," said Father McGooch. "I am on the Board of... hang on one second."

The priest grunted sweatily and ejaculated into his robes.

"As I was saying, I am on the Board of Directors. Mr. Bunn, do you have any experience running a publishing house?"

"No," replied Harry.

"That's fine. We don't know what the hell we're doing anymore anyway. You want the job?"

"Fuck yes, I do."

"Done," said the preacher. "Welcome to Kids First! Publishing."

"You two are awful," spat Robert.

"No one's denying that," said Harry.

"You're going to be rich now, Harry," said Father McGooch. "You don't need to talk to poor people like him anymore."

"Neat."

***

The book, *I Found Jesus*, sold eight hundred billion copies. The entire Amazon rainforest basin was razed for paper for the third printing alone. J.K. Rowling wrote a spin-off series of six books, including the best-selling *Harry Potter and the Anal Fissures of Azkaban*. All seven books were turned into two movies each. Southern California actually sank into the ocean under the weight of all the cash money they made.

Father Giuseppe McGooch and Harry Bunn became rich enough to privately purchase all of the third-world countries in the world. They promptly turned them all into illegal sex-tourism traps, then paid the governments of the world enough money to make the forced prostitution of underage boys not-illegal anymore.

They made so much more money from the sex tourism that they were able to start buying first-world countries.

Rachel Bunn never did regain the use of her legs, but it didn't matter, because she was married to a stupidly rich publishing magnate and didn't need to do shit for herself anymore. Plus, Harry was able to jump the line of scientific advancement and get a pair of cybernetic prosthetics invented for his wife, solely so they could fuck standing up in their vault full of gold.

Robert January died penniless and alone, suffocating on his own vomit after eating some bad sushi from the gas station at which he worked.

The end.

Because the world is a terrible, horrible place.

Essential Fluids
by Johnny Ramrod

The producer, Ted "Fire Arms" Gaboa, sprinkled sand onto the one room set of *Essential Fluids*. Dusty Bazooms stood off in the corner, toweling herself off from her last scene. Buck Johnson spun around in the make-up chair, waiting for Ted to affix a dollar store mustache underneath his nose. The director, Newark Jones, and the cameraman, Freddy Wharts, discussed how the beach scene was going to be shot.

"So," said Newark, "we're gonna to start with both of them in the shot and then when Buck whips it out you walk behind him and start filmin' from over his shoulda."

"But won't I be facing away from the backdrop?"

"Yes, Freddy. But if you're doin' your job well you'll have the camera on Dusty for the majority of the time."

"But what if I fuck up?"

"We'll worry about that when it happens. You just better be proficient in the editing booth."

"I'm not."

"Well then don't fuck this shit up."

"I'm not doing no fecal play!" yelled Dusty from across the set. "I haven't worked in this industry for thirty years to be pooped on by some new guy."

"We're not talkin' 'bout feces," said Newark. "And mind ya business."

"How is gettin' deuced on not my business?"

Freddy continued, "Why can't I just film it from Dusty's perspective?"

"Because if you were watchin' this at home it would look like Buck was plowin' the viewer. Dudes ain't gonna want to be seein' that."

"Some would."

"And they would probably disapprove of the huge melons and female moaning in this picture."

"I don't know. The gays are pretty open-minded."

"True, but they're not the target demographic we're aimin' for here. Speaking of, shouldn't we be filmin' something by now?"

Newark looked over at Ted, who was adjusting his newly created sand dunes into the shape of genitalia.

"Ted! What the fuck are you doin'?"

"Making a giant sand dong," replied Ted.

"Might I ask why?"

"To help prop up Buck and Dusty."

"Now that's thinking!" said Buck, still sitting in the make-up chair and still with a naked upper lip. "By the way, I overheard something about fecal play? Am I dropping something off at the silicon valley in this scene?"

"No!" screamed Newark. "There's no shit in this movie!"

"Great," said Buck with angry disappointment. "I don't know if I'm comfortable with that."

"Whatever," said Newark, now turning his attention back to Ted and his sand wangs and whatnots. "Why is the tip facin' down?"

"So it looks like it's banging one of them," answered Ted.

"And if it's Buck?"

Ted thought about it for a moment and said, "It'll be funny?"

"Jesus fucking Christ! Why is everyone so intent on turnin' this into a gay porno?"

"Listen, don't get all snippy with me, Newark. I'm financing this thing. I can make it whatever I want to make it."

"But the distributor only does hetero."

"Good point. No sandy johnsons then," Ted said, crushing the phallus with his feet. "Happy now?"

"Filled with glee. Now help Buck with that stupid stash so we can begin."

"I, uh, don't mean to interrupt, but did someone mention my sister?" asked Buck.

"Who the fuck," said Newark, "is your fuckin' sister?"

"Sandy. Someone said Sandy Johnson. She's in porn too. Now that I'm down for."

"Buck," said Newark. "No." He stopped to think about it. "Is she hot? Wait, don't answer that. We're not goin' there."

Buck Johnson and Dusty Bazooms sat in about an inch of sand, wearing a yellow Speedo and a green bikini respectively. Newark stood beside them explaining the scene and what was to be accomplished.

"Okay, guys. One more to go after this. You're gonna start off talking about how hot it is and all that."

"I could say something about having sand in my butt," said Dusty.

"Good. Good. Buck, you'll respond with somethin' about lendin' a hand or whateva. Then you both laugh, flirt a little, start kissin' and so on. At this point, Dusty, you'll stop, start panickin' and say, 'Oh no! We forgot the sunscreen!' Buck, you'll respond with a smile and say, 'Not to worry! I've got somethin' you can apply.' At this point you'll drop trou and do your thing. Got it?"

"Yup," said the actors.

"Good," said the director. "Camera?"

"Rolling."

"Great. Then start fuckin'."

And so they did, tearing through the "plot" in about thirty seconds and then really laying into the naked grinding. About six minutes into the cocksucking portion of the movie, Dusty pulled Buck's johnson from her mouth and said, "Stop, stop."

"What the fuck is it?" barked Newark.

"I've got sand in my butt," replied the adult film actress, "like, for reals though. It's super uncomfortable."

"You've gotta be shittin' me."

"I'm not doing no fecal play, Newark! We're not going over this again!"

"That's – It's a figure of speech." He shook his head. "Fine, we'll take five so Dusty can clear her shitter. Everyone cool with that?"

Everyone on the set nodded in agreement. Dusty let go of Buck's cock and walked over to the full length mirror stashed out-of-camera in the corner of the room. Buck, watching as Dusty bent over and shoved a few fingers up her ass, masturbated slowly. Then less slowly.

"Slow it down, Buck," said Newark. "We ain't filming right now and we need your full load for the money shot."

"Oh, right," said the porn star, slowing his roll once again. "You know, if you'd hire a proper fluffer I wouldn't have to do this myself."

"You know how much fluffers pull in?" asked Ted. "We can't afford that."

"Shit!" yelped Dusty.

"What is it now?" asked Newark.

"I'm... stuck. My hand is stuck up my ass."

"You're kidding me."

"No, I'm not," replied the actress, still doubled over and trying awkwardly to turn around. "I'm up to my wrist and I can't get it back out."

"Shit," continued Newark. "Eh, fuck it. Freddy, start rolling again. There's gotta be some kinda market for this."

"It really hurts."

"Then there's definitely a market."

"That's fucked up, man," said Freddy, reluctantly lifting the camera to his shoulder.

"Yes it is."

Suddenly Dusty started screaming. She finally managed to remove her arm from her butthole. Unfortunately, her hand did not come along with it.

"Oh my fucking Christ," said Buck.

"What the shit..." said Newark.

"I think she needs medical attention," said Freddy.

"AAAAAAAAAAAAAAAAAAAAAAAAAAAAAAAAAAA
AAAAAAAAAAAAAAAAAAAAAAAAAAAAAAAAAAA
AAAAAAAAAAAAAAAAAAAAAAAAAAAAAAAAAAA

AAAAAAAAAAAAAAAAAAAAAAAAAAAAAAAAAAAAAA
AAAAAAAAAAAAAAAAAAAAAAAAAAAAAAAAAAAAAA
AAAHHHHHHHH!!!!!!" said Dusty.

She fell to the ground, pulling her bleeding stump to her busty chest.

"Thank God I didn't stick my dick in there yet," said Buck.

"It wasn't my ass! I didn't do this!" shouted the actress. "I think the sand... I think it's AAAAAAAAAAAAAAAAAAAAAAAAAAAAAAAAAAAAAA AAAAAAAAAAAAAAAAHHHHH!!!!!"

A geyser of blood erupted from her ass like a volcano on steroids. The force was so powerful, her body was actually being pushed across the floor. She slammed into the wall and broke her neck.

"Oh my fucking Christ," said Buck.

"What the shit..." said Newark.

"I think she needs medical attention," said Freddy.

"I think she's dead."

She was indeed dead. This did not stop the bleeding. Somehow it made it worse. The blood was shooting up and out of her and then falling down on the men like God was having a particularly bad period and was fresh out of pads and underpants.

"Oh shit," said Buck, remarkably quietly given the shouting everyone else was doing.

"What? What is it now?" barked Newark.

"I think it *is* the sand," he said. "I can't move."

The producer, director and cameraman turned to look at Buck. His legs appeared to have dissolved up to his knees.

"Why the fuck didn't you say something sooner?!" asked Ted.

"Or, y'know, move out of the fuckin' sand?" added Newark.

"I don't –" Buck fell over, dead from blood loss, before he could finish his explanation. As with Dusty, this did not deter the bleeding at all. The room had six inches of standing plasma in it at this point.

"We should probably leave," said Freddy, dropping his camera.

"Yeah, I, uh," stammered Newark, "sorry your movie's fucked, Ted."

"Whatever, let's get the fuck out of here."

The trio tried to turn, but the blood was up to their knees now. It was difficult to move.

"Shit."

"Fuck."

"Oh God."

Within moments, the porn star's thankfully STD-free blood was waist high on the three men. The healthiness, of the serum though, was little consolation to them.

"We are gonna drown here," said Freddy. "I never should of taken this job!"

"Yeah, well," began Newark, "glarbleglugglugglarp."

The blood had all but filled the room at this point. All three men had drowned, just as Freddy predicted. That was pretty much that.

Three weeks later, the bodies were found, trapped in a studio set full of congealed blood. After the five of them were chiseled out, one of the rescuers found the video camera. Freddy had left it running.

The ensuing movie was marketed as a snuff film and did very well for itself among individuals who like that sort of thing. The fact that there was more than one person who purchased it was proof enough for the distributor, Ass-to-Grave Productions, that mankind was doomed. Thankfully, they had begun preparations for this long ago.

Knowing full well the industry there were in, AGP had set for themselves a very, very low bar of what was acceptable. Two porn stars dying by way of magic, evil sand and three adult film crew members drowning in blood was specifically that bar. Once it happened, AGP executed a computer program named FUCK. On the sale of the snuff film's three thousandth copy, a switch would automatically be thrown, detonating a hydrogen bomb big enough to destroy the world.

Daniel Azucar, a reporter for Minneapolis' local NPR affiliate, was the man who purchased the fateful copy of the film. It was for a report he was working on, regarding the kinds of people who watch snuff films and how they're not all terrible. All the evidence he had gathered thus far was proving his theory totally incorrect. He had hoped that by his purchasing a copy of *Essential Fluids* purely for research he'd be able to justify running the story anyway.

He was wrong.

Daniel Azucar blew up the world in a maelstrom of fire and agony.

Way to fucking go, Daniel.

Asshole.

For the Children

by Sally Mustang-Leibowitz-Morgan-Jones-Washington-
Lee-Redbone, MFA, DDS

Billy, Timmy, Mary and Big Jim, four precocious fifth-
graders, stood in front of the dumpster behind Tug and
Jug, the world's first sperm donor clinic and coffee shop in
one. If the rumors in school were true, inside this ordinary
looking dumpster, this simple, everyday trash bin, this
humdrum, commonplace waste receptacle, was another
world. A fantasy world of goblins, demons and other
mythical creations. A refuge from reality. A safe haven
from the world of endless shit they all lived in.

Slowly, hesitantly, and with great anticipation and hope,
Billy put a hand on the dumpster's lid. The others watched.
Slowly, hesitantly, and with great anticipation and hope,
Billy lifted the lid. He looked inside.

"Do you see anything?" asked Mary.

"Is it the magical world they say it is?" asked Big Jim.

"Nope," said Billy. "Just another dumpster filled with
used condoms and coffee filters."

"Nuts," said Timmy. "I really thought this was the
one."

"Hey, wait…" Billy stood on his toes and looked
deeper into the dumpster. "I think something's moving in
there."

74

"Really?" asked Mary, jumping to his side and likewise peering inside.

"No, wait, I think it's just a rat."

"Nuts," repeated Timmy.

"Do you think those non-orphaned, above-poverty-level jerks at school just lied to us?" asked Big Jim. "Do you think there's not really a magical world in any of these dumpsters?"

"I don't know," said Billy. "But we can't give up hope."

"Actually," said a voice from behind the children, "you probably should."

Billy, Timmy, Mary and Big Jim, four precocious fifth-graders, were summarily and brutally raped and murdered in front of the dumpster behind Tug and Jug, by John Jacob Jingleheimersmith, the man that police would later call The Axe-Handle Sodomist, a name given to Jingleheimersmith for his signature "finishing move" of roughly separating the lower torso and buttock from the rest of his victim's body with the dull, rusted blade of an eighteenth century farming axe and then impaling the axe handle into the anus of the victim, leaving the bloody axe head gleaming in the moonlight. The rumors in school were emphatically not true, the dumpster was full of nothing but semen and lies, and the children found no refuge from reality.

Although the kids did finally escape the world of endless shit they all lived in.

Kind of.

That's something, right?

Really, John Jacob Jingleheimersmith is a hero, if you think about it.

I mean, they say in a mad world, only the mad are truly sane. And this is one fucked up world, isn't it? The least someone can do is try to remedy that, right?

I'm going to go rape and murder some children.

One Sexy Leafblower
by Ben Dover, Jr.

Pablo's monitor exploded in a shower of sparks and loud noises; what was left of the monitor erupted into flames. Pablo tilted his head.

Trevor rolled his chair over from the neighboring cubicle to investigate the kerfuffle.

"What'd you do?" he asked.

"Nothing," replied Pablo.

"That doesn't look like nothing."

"I think my brain did it. I looked at it and then it blew up and then it caught on fire."

"So clearly you'd come to the assumption that you have super powers."

The fire started swirling in a counterclockwise motion. It began to grow in height, finally stopping at about six feet. And then it changed to a deep purple color.

"Well that's different," said Trevor.

"Very," said Pablo.

The office was very small and had only about a dozen or so employees. There were more at one point, but Trevor had been dabbling in cannibalism for most of the past year. He had hoped that the company would consistently replenish the employee ranks, supplying him with a never ending buffet of temps and other assorted desk monkeys, but Trevor had started his people-eating experiment with Human Resources. And with Betty gone, no one was legally allowed to hire anyone new – not even a new HR representative. Trevor never was one to think ahead.

While there was no hard evidence that Trevor had been devouring his coworkers for the last ten months – this is why he wasn't in jail – the remaining employees of GeneriCo nonetheless suspected that he was behind all the disappearances and all the empty bottles of barbecue sauce in the kitchen. As such, they all kept a wide berth from Trevor and were therefore not present to see what fell out of the purple fire-tornado atop Pablo's desk.

The tiny creature landed limply on the desk with a squishy thud. It looked like a deformed cherub made of butter. The thing lay there for a moment before sitting up, shaking its horned head and then staring at Pablo and Trevor.

"What the hell is that?" asked Pablo.

"Looks like a demon," answered Trevor.

"Guess I have a portal to Hell in my cube then."

"Guess so."

"Now what?"

"I'm going to poke it," said Trevor, taking a step forward.

"OK, sure," said Pablo, staring at his co-worker with some concern. "Have fun with that. I'm going to find another monitor." He exited the cubicle.

Trevor stood next the creature; the demon looked him dead in the eyes. Trevor extended his index finger and moved his hand closer. Slowly. Ever so slowly. When he was about an inch away from its nose the creature lunged forward and bit off the tip of Trevor's finger.

"You motherfucker!" shouted Trevor.

He punched the demon in the face.

Then he grabbed the keyboard from Pablo's desk and proceeded to bludgeon the demon with it, little plastic letters flying everywhere.

"Ow, OW!" said the demon.

"Fuck you!" said Trevor.

The keyboard cracked in half. No longer useful as an implement of pain, or typing, Trevor tossed it to the ground and grabbed a letter opener. The demon, bloodied and bruised, looked at Trevor, looked at the letter opener, then looked back at Trevor and then he raised his middle fingers and exploded in a spray of purple glitter.

Pablo returned at that moment with a cardboard box that had the word "MONITOR" written on one side of it and a drawing of a monitor on the opposite side.

"This was all the IT department had. Something about cutbacks and fucking my dog. I don't know. I hate those guys," he said, before noticing the letter opener in Trevor's hand. "Uh, you okay?"

Trevor, startled out of his rage, said, "Oh… yeah. No problem. The demon-thingy vanished."

"Why? You didn't eat him did you?"

"The thought had crossed my mind, but no. I went to poke it when it bit off part of my finger. Then I punched it."

"You punched it?"

"Yeah."

"A creature from Hell. You punched a creature from Hell?"

"Yes, damn it. Pay attention! Then I beat it with your keyboard. I'm sorry, by the way," said Trevor, motioning towards the alphabet scattered throughout the cubicle.

"Oh…"

"Then I grabbed this pointy thing, but before I could stab the motherfucker, it flipped me off and vanished."

"Aw. Now what are we gonna do?"

"Work? Get medical attention?"

"That's boring."

"What?" barked Trevor. "What do you know about boring? You left to get office equipment with a squishy hellspawn on your desk! You showed zero interest in any of this!"

"I thought it'd still be here when I got back!"

"You seriously want a demon running around the office?"

"Sure," Pablo said with a shrug. "Give us something to do."

"Fair enough," said Trevor, likewise shrugging. "I'll get you another one. Forgot to get you something for your birthday anyway. I'm going in."

"Going where now?"

"Into the purple tornado of doom or whatever you want to call it."

"You're going to Hell?"

"Guess my parents were right after all."

"All right. You do that. I'm going to get a new keyboard from those IT assholes."

"YOU JUST SAID WORK WAS BORING!"

"Yeah, well –" Pablo shoved Trevor into the spinning wind funnel of purple terror.

Unfortunately for everyone involved – mostly just Pablo – Trevor's belongings didn't make it through the spinning portal. His clothes, the thirty-five cents in his pocket and the letter opener bounced off the purple vortex and fell onto Pablo's desk. Trevor himself went through just fine, however. Which meant that for a brief second, in between his clothing collapsing and his body disappearing into Hell, Trevor was completely nude. And given that he had been shoved in backwards, this meant Pablo got an eyeful of full frontal Trevor.

Pablo was momentarily blinded.

***

Trevor landed in Hell, hard on his ass and smack dab in the middle of Satan's backyard. His naughty bits flopping around dangerously, Trevor looked for his pants but found nothing besides surprisingly moist grass. He ripped a few handfuls out and pressed it against his privates. The majority of it stuck.

It was at this moment that the Devil emerged from his log cabin and saw the intruder defiling his prize-winning lawn.

"The fuck you doing, boy?" asked Satan in a thick Texas drawl.

Trevor immediately crapped himself.

***

Meanwhile, back at the office, Pablo had regained his sight and started conducting an experiment. He picked Trevor's shirt off of the desk and threw it at the portal. It went through.

"Huh," he said.

He picked up both socks and chucked them at the purple tornado. The same result.

"That's stupid."

Nonetheless, Pablo stripped off his clothes, threw them through the portal and then followed after them.

"You just going to poop all over my lawn?" the Devil barked.

"Fertilizer...?" Trevor suggested meekly.

"Oh," said Satan, scrunching his face slightly. "You're that new gardener! I thought you was coming tomorrow. Not too sure I agree with your methods, but you've been highly recommended to so I'll take your word for it."

"OK, thanks."

Satan lead Trevor around the property, showing him the areas that needed the most work. Halfway through the tour, Pablo and his clothes appeared, landing awkwardly on the damned grass. Seeing Satan talking to Trevor at the edge of the lawn, Pablo quickly gathered up his clothes and ran into the Devil's cabin before either of them saw him.

"And these here are my prized begonias," continued Satan.

"They are lovely," replied Trevor.

"Damn right they are. They've won first place at the annual Hell Fun Fair for the past six hundred years running."

"So I take it I should take extra care not to run them over with the lawnmower?"

"That would be preferred, yes."

"OK."

"OK."

Satan stood with his hands on his hips, proudly beaming at the flowers. Through the triangle-shaped gap beneath the Devil's armpit, Trevor could see Pablo ransacking the log cabin. Pablo appeared to be taking out a lifetime of bottled-up anger on Satan's porcelain pig statues. Satan noticed Trevor staring off into his home and turned to look at what had caught his gardener's attention. Furious, the Dark Lord stormed inside and confronted the pig destroyer.

"What in the fuck do you think you're doing, son?"

Pablo thought about it for a moment, still holding a porcelain pig statue above his head.

"Boss," he said, letting the pig fall, "you didn't get the email?"

"What email?"

"The email from Martha. Said she was sending me down here to fix up your place a bit. Said that you were a bit too much of a neat freak and needed to 'free the beast within' a little more. If I'm remembering that correctly."

"Really?"

"Yes. You were copied on it."

"My Wi-Fi has been a little spotty recently."

"Fucking Comcast."

"You'd have thunk she would've mentioned it in our weekly meeting."

"Probably just slipped her mind. You know how busy she is. Almost as busy as you."

"That she is," said Satan. "Guess I'll leave you to it then. Martha ain't done me wrong yet."

"That she hasn't."

"All right, well," said Satan, "guessing I'll be off to the store then. I'm having some guests come by tonight. Probably why Martha sent you."

"Oh, yeah, of course. I won't be long."

"Oh, one more thing, son. Can I ask you to do me a favor?"

"Sure thing," said Pablo.

"Can you keep an eye on that pantsless gardener out there? He's good, but I saw him rubbing grass on his crotch."

"Oh my."

"Yeah, just keep an eye on him and make sure he doesn't screw my leafblower."

"You got it."

***

After smashing a few more pigs, Pablo walked outside to Satan's backyard and found Trevor screwing the Devil's leafblower.

"Dude," said Pablo.

"Almost done," said Trevor.

"DUDE."

"What?"

"Seriously?"

"Man, I'm already in hell," said Trevor, thrusting furiously. "So, why the fuck not, right?"

"I... I don't even know how to respond to that."

"She instigated it."

"What?"

"Just give me five, six minutes and I'll meet you back in the office."

"Oh, OK, sure."

"Something wrong?" asked the continually humping Trevor.

"Not really. Just a little surprised you want to go back so soon."

"I don't. I thought you did."

"Not really."

"What do you want to do then?"

"I don't know. I guess we could find that demon thing from the office."

"It exploded," said Trevor, breathing heavily. "You still want another one?"

"Meh."

"We could pick on Hitler?"

"I suppose."

"Hold up a second," interrupted Trevor, before tightly gripping the side of the leafblower and moaning softly. His knees buckled slightly.

"Woo!" he continued, disengaging himself from the landscaping appliance. "That is one sexy leafblower."

"You have some problems."

"Undoubtedly. I think the heat's getting to me."

"I don't think it's the heat."

"Don't judge me. I've seen you hump washing machines."

"I was drunk!"

"You don't drink."

"When I'm drunk I do."

"OK, well, whatever, hypocrite Harry. What about that thing you wanted to do?"

"I told you I'm done humping washing machines!"

"Other definition of 'do.' And a more vague definition of 'thing.'"

"Oh, right, well..." said Pablo. "I guess I'd like to find the inventor of the nine to five workday and kick him in the nuts."

"I think we can do that. You sure he's in Hell?"

"Wouldn't he have to be?"

"Point."

"Set and Match."

Trevor had a perplexed expression on his face. "Did you just make a tennis reference?"

"I believe I might have," said Pablo.

"I was not aware you even knew OF tennis."

"I played it in a video game once."

***

"We've been wandering around Hell for days," said Trevor, still wearing nothing but a little bit of now crusty grass. "Do we even know this guy's name?"

"I don't need to tell you what I do and don't know."

"If you don't, then I'm gonna give in to my boredom and go home!"

"Oh, then no. I don't know his name."

88

"The fuck are we doing then?"

"I suggested holding up a sign that—"

"No. Enough of your sign idea."

"But—"

"Walking around with a sign that asks 'Did you invent the nine to five workday?' wouldn't work. There's just too many people here and most of them are liars."

"Yeah, well, it's better than nothing, Mr. … Nothing," Pablo taunted. Sort of.

"Fine. How about we… just go around kicking everyone in the nuts?" Trevor offered.

"Yeah, OK."

"Was that sarcastic? Or are you actually agreeing?"

"I'm actually agreeing." And with that, Pablo kicked Trevor in the nuts.

***

Three hours later, Trevor and Pablo – bruised, walking funny and tired of kicking one another in the testicles – set out on their mission. Their first stop: Hell's public pool.

Well, no, that's not true. There first stop was Hitler's bungalow. Then they got a sno-cone. Then they went back to Hitler's place and kicked him in the balls some more. THEN they went to Hell's public pool.

"Not that crowded," said Trevor upon entering the pool area.

"A slide!" shouted Pablo. Immediately he stripped down to his boxers and climbed up the slide's ladder.

"Idiot! The pool is filled with lava!"

But Trevor's warning was too late. Pablo slid face first into the molten rock.

There was a lot of screaming. And laughing. The screaming coming from Pablo and the laughing from Trevor and the lifeguard. The lifeguard, despite his title, made no effort to help Pablo. In fact, he pulled out his cell phone and began recording Pablo's agonized flailing.

"Why would he do that?" asked the snickering lifeguard.

"He really likes slides," replied Trevor, shrugging.

"OH MY FUCKING GOD THIS HURTS HELP ME WHY ARE YOU LAUGHING OH MY SWEET JESUS I THINK I JUST LOST MOST OF MY SKIN I HATE YOU ALL STOP LAUGHING HELP ME OH GOD IT HURTS HOLY FUCKING EVERYTHING IT HURTS"

Eventually Pablo, skinless, made his way out of the pool and over towards Trevor.

"OK, I'm ow going home," he said between painful convulsions. "Well, to the hospital first ow and then home. I think my blood ow sugar is ow dangerously low."

"Plus you don't have any skin."

"Yeah, that ow ow ow too."

Trevor bent down and picked up Pablo's pants. "You mind?"

"No. Go ow ahead. I don't think clothing would ow FUCK ow be a wise choice right now."

"Thanks."

"You coming with?"

"Don't think so. Satan's expecting me back in the morning."

"You could still come ow back to the ow office."

"Eh," Trevor said with a shrug. "I promised Ethel I'd take her out to dinner."

"Ethel?"

"The leafblower."

"The ow leafblower?"

"I really like her. I think we have a real chance at making this work."

"She's a ow piece of gardening ow FUCK equipment."

"Your MOM is a piece of gardening equipment."

"Yeah, but..."

"Tell her I said hi."

"No. Mom jokes ow aside. Ethel ow is ow mechanical. You know ow this right?"

"Yes."

"Okay, just ow making sure you ow haven't ow ow ow MOTHERFUCKER lost your mind."

Trevor and Pablo looked at each other. Trevor with Pablo's pants cinched at the waist; Pablo without any skin, hoping from one foot to the other in pain.

"So," said Trevor.

"So," said Pablo. "Ow."

"I, uh, I guess this is it."

"Looks like."

"Have fun with your boring life. Tell Nate I quit. Then tell everyone else in the office I hate them. And don't let anyone you like in my cubicle. There's… things set up in there that I forgot how to disarm."

"Will do," said Pablo. "Have ow fun with your ow, uh, leafblower."

"She has a name, damn it!"

"Yes, well, I don't ow care." Pablo began limping across the pool deck, toward the gate.

"Are you really going to walk all the way back to the portal at Satan's with no skin?"

"I don't think I have any ow ow FUCKING FUCKS other option."

"I have an idea," said Trevor.

He turned to the lifeguard – who had been standing there the whole time, trying to upload the video of Pablo screaming to Hell's YouTube – and punched him. He punched him hard. Trevor kept punching the lifeguard until he exploded in a spray of yellow glitter. In the space formerly occupied by the lifeguard a spinning yellow vortex emerged.

"There you go," said Trevor, covered in yellow demon blood. "One portal back to the office."

"I don't remember it ow happening that way the first–"

"Yeah, well, I do."

"You sure it goes ow to the office?"

"Only one way to find out."

Trevor grabbed Pablo by his skinless shoulders and threw him into the portal.

***

The portal didn't transport Pablo to the office. It dropped him unceremoniously in between two teams of high school students in the middle of a week-long dodgeball tournament. The bodies of dehydrated and concussed students lay everywhere, twitching, moaning, screaming. No one even noticed that Pablo didn't belong. He was pelted with rubber balls for days. Pablo's screams could be heard for miles... above and below ground.

"You hear something, honey?" asked Trevor.

The leafblower – resting at the side of the yard, a flower in its exhaust vent – did not respond.

"Huh, guess it was nothing."

Trevor began whistling and went back to tending Satan's begonias.

Moose Cleaning
by S.N. Atch and S.N. Iff

The sign was on the side of the road, clear as day:

Moose Cleaning
$45

"That can't be for a real moose," pondered Ashley.

"Why not? Mooses need to be clean," countered Hans.

"I guess so. Should we?"

"Should we what?"

"Buy a moose, sully it and then come back here to clean that bastard up."

"Where would we go to buy a moose?"

"Craigslist?"

"Makes sense."

***

By the end of the afternoon Ashley Pretzelburger-Dubblegruber and Hans Dubblegruber were the proud owners of Gustav the moose. And just like the ad said, Gustav came fully aroused and ready to go. His dick barely fit through the door of their cabin.

"Why did you pick this one?" asked Hans, winded from the effort of forcing a horny moose into his house.

"First of all, we picked each other," Ashley corrected. "You know that moment when you see a dog in the pound and you both know you've found your best friend? Well, that happened here. I saw his picture, masturbated on it for a bit and knew right then and there."

"You what?"

"I strummed off for a bit. Set a record too."

"What for quickness?"

"Yeah. Not to mention amount of times and distance."

"Distance?" questioned Hans.

"Yeah, I was in the den and... well, you need a new computer monitor."

"But mine was across the room!"

"Yeah, I shot a hole right through it. Plus the 'water' damage."

"Oh, God, no, not the chair!"

"Yes, the chair. I know you loved it like an incestuous brother, but that chair is drowned now. It drowned harder than your actual incestuous brother."

"Sweet Jesus!"

"I'll say. I haven't cum that hard since my first communion."

"Pardon?"

"What'd ya, fart?"

"No. What happened during your first comm–"

"Speaking of," interrupted Ashley, "Gustav and I have something to discuss in the other room." She grabbed the majestic beast by the beaver basher and led it into the bedroom.

***

Sixty-nine mind-shattering hours later, Gustav exited with a cigarette in his mouth. He brought one of his front hooves up to his mouth, removed the fag and blew out a thick stream of smoke.

"Hans!" bellowed the woodland creature, calling across the empty cabin. "Where you at, bud? Ashley, uh, needs some help."

Hans, in his tighty-whiteys and on a pogo stick, bounced up to Gustav from his makeshift campsite outside – the only place he could go to avoid his wife's moaning and the moose's groaning, and keep his ears from bleeding and his balls from exploding – and asked, "Is everything ok?"

The moose replied: "That bitch is a freak!"

"Well, yeah."

Hans ditched the pogo stick and entered his bedroom. Even with his prodigious knowledge of Ashley's proclivities, he could not fathom what might have taken place to leave his wife covered in what seemed liked over a dozen different bodily fluids and torn from snatch to crack. And even a bit up her back.

"Are you okay?" asked the mildly concerned husband.

"Never been better," replied the preposterously satisfied wife, resting on her knees and her rug-burned face, still squirting like a clown's seltzer bottle.

"I can see your insides."

"How inside?"

"I'm pretty sure I can see your lunch."

"Joke's on you! All I had for lunch was moose drip."

"Then when did you eat pizza?"

"Brunch?"

"OK then. I can see your brunch."

"Well, damn. Not that I'm surprised," she continued, speaking mostly into the comforter. "That moose has a gigantic cock. I'm not even sure where he pulled it from. Poor thing suffocated while inside me, but what a way to go. Oh, the moose has an enormous penis, too."

"So... that thing in the corner then? It's..."

"The rooster that died inside of my cunt, yeah."

Hans fell over backwards into a pile of what he hoped, but knew full well wasn't, implausibly thick whip cream.

***

Hans Dubblegruber woke up a few minutes later in the passenger seat of his car, his wife in the driver's seat and his sister-husband-moose in all of the backseats.

"Where are we going?" he asked.

"I need a bath," answered Gustav.

"Hey, since when can you talk, by the way? I don't remember that being in the ad."

"I think I banged that into him," explained Ashley.

"How?"

"Well, I took his wang and put it inside me and bounced around a bit. Then all of a sudden he started talking. I told you my vag was magic."

"Sorry to break it to you," chimed in Gustav, "but that's not how it happened. I was born with this ability."

"Yeah, bullshit," replied Ashley. "Like that makes any sense. Magic pussy for the win! Eat it everyone who said it wasn't!"

Across the country, millions of men and women suddenly had the urge to dive into some muff cabbage.

The trio arrived at the moose cleaners, pulling up right outside the front door. The Dubblegrubers exited, entered, walked across the waiting room and up to the counter, where they rang a delightfully antiquated bell for service. All the while Gustav attempted to extricate himself from the backseat of their car.

A young man shot up from behind the counter.

"Bonjour," he said.

"Hi!" said a chipper and still fluid-covered Ashley. "We'd like you to clean our moose, Gustav.

"Yeah, sure," said Cousteau the counter attendee, who happened to be an art history major who, after ten years, was still looking for a job in his field. Poor bastard. "That's kind of what we do."

Cousteau exited from behind the counter, and then the storefront, and walked over to Gustav, who had finally pulled himself free of the car seat. Patting the moose gently on the antlers, the cleaner said, "This way, boy."

Gustav, stricken with a sudden and blinding rage, stood up on his hind legs and revealed his massive meat thermometer.

"WHO THE FUCK DO YOU THINK YOU'RE CALLING 'BOY,' NUT-SCRUBBER?!"

His wang wanged the French-Canadian wang in his wang. Cousteau doubled over and the moose towered over the man who was about to be scrubbing his under carriage.

"Turn around, little man!"

"I don't think I want to," he coughed.

"TURN THE FUCK AROUND!"

Cousteau turned around.

"Now drop your khakis!"
Already bent over from the wang wanging, Cousteau did as he was told and prepared his anus for what was sure

to be one of the most God-awful experiences he'd ever had the pleasure of maybe living through.

Gustav's engorged pleasure club stood throbbing at the ready. The customer service representative's tiny pink butthole quivered in both fear and morbid curiosity.

"There's just no way that thing is going to fit in there," said Hans.

"Shit," said Ashley, "I bet it rips him it two. Which would clearly be the most satisfying outcome."

"Fucking French-Canadians."

The moose pushed his way inside the counter jockey, significantly tearing Cousteau's starfish beyond all hope of repair and, honestly, identification. Still the moose went deeper. All three feet of the beast's custard launcher squeezed its way inside the poor boy's body.

"I can feel my insides rupturing!" cried the shish kabob meat.

"Yeah, more dirty talk!" bellowed the skewer.

Gustav began thrusting rhythmically as the married couple – and the corporate security guys on the other end of the moose cleaners' surveillance cameras – watched. His massive moose meatballs smashed against the back of his victim's legs. The slapping noise could be heard from miles away. The bruises were already deep purple. Cousteau's tiny, pink worm flopped in the breeze, showing no sign of arousal.

"Oh. God. I. Can. Taste. It," Cousteau said in between slammings.

"Damn right, you can," said the majestic beast, picking up speed. "Almost there."

"I can't watch this," said Hans, putting up a hand and walking away.

"But it's about to get really interesting," said Ashley, never taking her eyes from the moose-on-man action.

"Nope, getting a soda," said Hans, facing away from all the action and entering the waiting room again.

"Here..." began the moose.

His front hooves dug deeper into the sides of his love slave.

"It..." he continued.

He planted his rear hooves for increased stability.

"Comes!"

"NOOOO–" screamed Cousteau as the moose's thundersword released its mighty load from deep within his chest, the sex gravy rocketing out of the French-Canadian's open mouth, right in the middle of his defiant exclamation. Ashley clapped her hands as she was once again bathed in Gustav's penis juices.

"I'm so wet right now," she cooed.

"I know it, baby," replied Gustav. "Give me five and we can – Hmm."
"Something wrong?"

"The moose cleaner guy... I think he's stuck."

Gustav swung his mighty wiener around. Cousteau, now deceased, barely budged.

"Try smacking it against the car."

"OK."

The moose did as instructed and smacked his French-Canadian-encased dick against the Dubblegruber's sedan. Cousteau's body snapped and purpled, the car rocked and dented, windows shattered, but the cleaning dude was still wedged pretty firmly on the moose's cock.

"No dice."

"Well, you better figure something out soon," replied Ashley. "The longer I see him on there, the less attracted I am to you."

"That doesn't seem fair."

"The fuck do I care? Fair," she scoffed. "Get that guy off your cock or we're through!"

Gustav banged his sausage around a few more times, shouting, "You think I want him on here?"

"You want? *You* want?! There you go again! Always your needs! What about me? Huh? What about what *I* want?!"

"You want me to get him off! That's what I'm trying to do!"
"Oh, so now it's about *his* sexual pleasure? Well, fuck you too then, Gustav! We're done!"

Ashley Pretzelburger-Dubblegruber pulled a sawed-off

shotgun from somewhere within her gaping lady-hole, put it against her chin and pulled the trigger, blowing her brains all over the moose cleaners' front window.

"HOLY SHIT!" barked Gustav, his cock finally going limp and releasing Cousteau's battered corpse to the dirty parking lot ground. "Hans! HANS!"

Hans, having just that moment returned from getting a soda from the fountain at the far end of the moose cleaners' waiting room, leaned against the doorframe and sipped at his straw.

With a shrug he said, "That bitch is a freak."

From behind Hans, another moose cleaner, this one named Gaston, fresh off his break, sighed deeply.

"Not again," he mumbled.

There's Something on the Wheel!
by H.R. Muffenstoeff

Peter Piper – older, whiter and jowlier than anyone else on the bus – was sitting with his head fully out of the window like a suicidal basset hound, trying to wake up. It had been a long trip already and it was only half over.

Adding to his problems, one of the front wheels was removing itself from the bus.

Bug-eyed, Peter ducked his head back into the bus, narrowly dodging decapitation by tire. But before he did, he spotted something darting back into the wheel well. Something that didn't belong. Something… green.

That could wait, though. There were more pressing matters at hand.

"The wheel came off!" he shouted, as crazed as he could manage.

"It's fine, sir," said Crystal, the stout, dreadlocked bus stewardess, already exasperated with him. "All our wheels run double for just such a situation."

"That seems awfully wasteful," replied Peter. "Is that why the ticket prices are so high?"

"The ticket prices are so high because we have to pay the drivers exceedingly well because no sane person would ever be a bus driver. And sanity is what we're all about."

"I remember that from your commercial."

"Also, you know, bus stewardesses."

"Oh, right. Yeah, most busses don't have those."

"They do not."

Peter Piper leaned back into his seat, his fear momentarily sated. Then something green darted past the window. Then another. He stuck his head out of the window to look.

"Holy nuts," he mumbled. "There's something on the wheel!"

He pulled his head back in and shouted the statement again at the top of his lungs.

"THERE'S SOMETHING ON THE WHEEL!"

He shoved his cranium back out the window, staring at the something. A little green something, hanging off the bus wheel like a tourist off the back of a trolley in San Francisco. The little green something was vaguely man-shaped, with a disproportionately large, egg-shaped torso and four spindly appendages. It looked like an angry frog, except it was wearing welding goggles. This despite the fact that he was tearing at the wheel with his long claws and not welding even a little.

"There's something on the wheel!" Peter shouted again, standing on his seat and pointing out the window. Crystal stood in the aisle, arms crossed across her prodigious bosom, gaze noticeably pissed off. Peter grabbed her by the shoulders. "There's something on the wheel!"

"There's lots of things on the wheel, sir," the bus stewardess explained, "it's not an autonomous system. It needs to be connected to the axle, which is in turn connected to the drive shaft —"

"No," he shouted, "not a wheel thing. A something else thing! It looks like – like – like a little green man on the wheel!"

"What are you on, sir?" said the stewardess sternly, hands on her hips, before adding softly, "And how much do you want for a couple hits?"

"There's a little green man on the wheel! Stick your head out the window and look!"

"No. I like my head on my neck where it is. We'll look when we pull over."

"By then it might be too late!"

"Too late for what? If there's something stuck on the wheel the worst we'll do is lose another tire and then we'll just pull over and fix it. The driver's a trained professional. You're treating this with an awful lot of urgency for a bus ride."

"You don't understand!"

Just then, the bus rocked. Through the windows the jowly man and the Rubenesque stewardess saw several more of the vehicle's wheels flying free.

"Oh, God, it's happening!" Peter shouted.

"What's happening? What are you talking about, sir?!"

Crystal grabbed the crazed passenger by his arm and spun him, pinning Peter's hand behind his back and pressing his face against the edge of the upholstered bench seat. The stewardess pulled a stainless steel shiv from her boot and held it against his ribcage.

"Under bus law, I'm authorized to use deadly force."

"It's the green men! They're dismantling the bus!"

She pressed the shiv harder against him, the freshly-sharpened blade cutting through his shirt and resting on his skin.

"Under bus law, I'm ordering you to give me some of whatever the hell you're smoking!"

"Really?" asked Peter, momentarily distracted from his tirade. "You can do that?"

"Oh, hell yeah. This job gets so boring. We had them add it to our contracts. We have a great union."

"Wouldn't being high get in the way of you doing your jobs?"

"Less than you'd expect."

Suddenly, a thick panel of bus roof rattled upward and tore off, sailing away on the wind. Peter and Crystal – and most of the other passengers who hadn't taken a handful of sleeping pills – looked up just in time to see the head of a little green man staring back at them.

"Son of a bitch!" shouted the stewardess, stabbing the shiv into Peter's sides.

"Ow! What the hell?!"

The gremlin disappeared.

"Oh, shit, sorry," said Crystal, removing the blade from the man's insides. She wiped the blood on her skirt and placed the makeshift knife back into her boots.

"You're not even going to sterilize it?"

"Why would I sterilize it? That's my stabbing knife, not my eating kni–"

"It was inside me!" shouted Peter.

"Maybe you should've been more coherent then!" She pressed his arm harder.

"You could've given me polio or –"

"We have a cure for that!"

"I was going to list mo–"

"Why would you even start with that, though?"

"It's not like it's a good disease or something!"

"It's extinct!"

"Eradicated!"

"What?"

"Eradicated when you're talking about diseases, extinct when –"

Several more chunks of roof tore off. Then a few windows and wall panels. Then the entirety of the front windshield was removed, sailing up over the bus and crashing down onto the highway behind it. The driver swerved the bus violently, the sudden assault of fresh air too much for his face to bear. The vehicle crashed through a wall and into a roadside diner. A ceiling fan crashed through the face of the driver and into the back of his seat.

The groggy, yet panicked, passengers began to get up.

They were immediately swarmed by the gremlins.

"Oh, god!"

The green, ovoid creatures began latching onto people's faces. The people began to scream and claw at the creatures.

One of the larger gremlins, bounding from chair back to chair back, leapt for Crystal's face. With the reflexes of a black belt on speed, she grabbed the creature by its thick neck.

"What do you want, you little, green asshole?!" she demanded.

"Our species is almost extinct!" the gremlin squeaked. "Hunted down to extinction by some kind of Jamaican predator from outer space! We –"

The stewardess pulled her shiv from her boot. "GET TO THE FUCKING POINT!"

"We need to repopulate!"

Crystal looked at all the faces. And all the undulating

green men on those faces.

"Oh, my god. You're –"

"THEY'RE RAPING MY FACE!" shouted Peter Piper, sprawled on the seat beside Crystal, his jowls flapping in rhythm with the gremlin humping his mouth.

"How does that even work?" asked the stewardess.

"Due to a quirk of evolution…" began the gremlin. "Look, it's involved. Do you really want me to get into it?"

"Not really, no." Crystal squished the gremlin in her ham-sized fist until the creature exploded. The stewardess immediately regretted the action, spitting chunks of green slime and viscera from her mouth. "That was gross."

"MY FACE IS STILL BEING RAPED HERE," Peter helpfully commented.

"Then shut your mouth, slut."

His eyes just visible behind the thrusting gremlin, Crystal could see that Peter was emotionally hurt. She, however, was out of fucks to give.

"Shift just ended," she explained. "I don't have to give a rat's ass about any of you anymore." From her other boot she pulled a pack of cigarettes and an expensive lighter.

Crystal strolled casually toward the back of the bus as chests burst open on either side of her, tiny, snarling, fuzzy gremlins exploding from the passengers' insides.

"BUT –" began Peter, his mouth full of gremlin genitalia.

111

"Call me when it's my problem," she said, throwing open the emergency door and hopping off the back of the bus.

***

Twenty minutes later, the next stewardess – or steward, as they case actually was – hopped aboard the bus/gremlin baby factory to start his shift.

"Sorry I'm late," he said, stepping through the front door of the bus and into what one would hope to be the world's largest gang rape. "It was hard to find you guys, what with the bus crashing into a diner and every–"

Only then did the steward, a mountain of a man named Norbert Gunderson, realize what he was looking at. He stood there in shock for a moment, then promptly ripped his tight, short pants off, revealing his Guinness record-holding manhood. Being a man of his size, he had long ago realized underwear was pointless. It only slowed him down.

Norbert bent down at the waist and unfastened the three clasps that held his gigantic penis to his tree trunk-like leg. The man meat immediately sprang upward, hitting the steward in the face a couple times before settling itself at a hundred degree angle. The man was, literally, a tripod.

"HEY!" Norbert shouted. All of the gremlins, continuing to hump away, turned their heads. The pantsless steward stared the green creatures down, growling, "Not on my bus."

Norbert Gunderson charged down the bus aisle, his enormous wiener bouncing from side-to-side against the seats. The steward was using his jumbo salami like a medieval lance, smacking face-rapists and paying customers alike as he moved. Gremlins flew from passengers' faces, falling to the ground or being tossed through the dismantled walls, streams of cum and spit trailing behind in their wake. The passengers, meanwhile, were just happy to have human genitalia slapped against them instead of the strange, green members currently penetrating their oral cavities.

Well, the handful of passengers that were still alive, that is.

Those that had already violently given birth to the next generation of face-fuckers were very much dead and continued to be, their hollowed-out torsos oozing blood and green pus. Not that this stopped the gremlins from continuing to have their way with them. In fact, the younger of the gremlins were using the corpses as practice dummies, ejaculating into the bodies and watching their gooey essence leak out of the chest cavities, dripping to the floor and hardening like a disgusting, unmarketable brand of quick-dry cement.

Undeterred, Norbert Gunderson made his way farther down the bus, his goal not so much saving the passengers as murdering gremlins. Like all bus stewards, he hated his job and the customers that came with it. He could give a fuck if they lived or died, as long as he got paid. Unlike other stewards, though, Norbert's parents had been raped to death by gremlins and he wasn't about to let that go unvengeanced.

Peter Piper, one of the surviving – and still being face-raped – passengers, didn't particularly care about the distinction.

Soon enough, Norbert reached Peter, swinging his magic johnson at the gremlin violating the man's face. The steward missed, though, hitting the passenger's ear with his mammoth wang. The large-cocked man tried again and again to free Peter's face of the fierce and ferocious fucker fucking his face, but the gremlin was too quick, leaping from orifice to orifice, shoving his green wang into every opening Peter Piper's skull had.

The steward, frustrated and furious, finally zeroed-in and came charging at the gremlin, his monolithic phallus in hand like a SWAT agent handling a battering ram. The penis and the face-raper collided with such force that the gremlin straight-up exploded.

The impact did not end well for Peter Piper, either.

"My brain!" shouted the bus passenger, before succumbing to – as the coroner would later describe it – "a shattered skull due to a really big fucking dong."

Norbert Gunderson, however, mourned not for the passenger he had just gratuitously murdered. The spirits of his forefathers overtaking him, the well-hung bus steward was overcome with a berserker fury and he penis-stabbed everyone and everything remaining on the vehicle.

***

Thirty disgusting, gore-filled minutes later, Norbert found himself sitting breathless on the back bumper of the bus, his Viking-ancestor-fueled blackout over and his rage boner subsiding. Around his feet were the corpses of several police officers, their heads all suspiciously full of dick-shaped holes.

"Oh, shit," muttered the man of the mammoth man-meat, "not again."

As sirens emerged off in the blackened distance, Norbert Gunderson ran back through the bus, rifling through the pockets of the passengers, shoving wallets and jewelry into the least cum-soaked messenger bag he could find. As he was about to leave, Norbert grabbed Peter Piper's phone, punched in a few numbers and called his girlfriend.

"Hey, babe," said the bus steward. "We're, uh, we're gonna have to move."

"You murdered some people with your dick again, didn't you?" replied Crystal.

"A lot of them were already dead," explained Norbert. "No thanks to you, I assume."

"You're an asshole. I don't even know why I put up with you."

"Because I can fuck your cooch by way of your throat."

"Oh, right," said the thick, insatiable bus stewardess, her hand unconsciously sliding toward her suddenly damp ladyparts. "OK, fine, I'll stay with you. How bad is this? Next state over or, like, Canada or something?"

"Canada? God no. These were just bus folk, Crystal. You know better than anyone that they don't count. A state or two between us and this shitshow should be fine."

"Cool. Meet me at the place. I'll bring the passports."

"Thanks, babe; you're a lifesaver. I love you."

"I love you too, Norby," replied Crystal. "Well, parts of you anyway."

Norbert ended the call. That was good enough for him. He hopped off the bus and disappeared into the night, heading toward his girlfriend and their safe house, hoping his days of gremlin genocide were finally at an end.

Barry Dingle vs. the Agents of P.O.o.P.
by Nathan W. Taynthoemer

Barry Dingle – in his late twenties, unemployed, single and wearing plaid pajama bottoms and a Teenage Mutant Ninja Turtles t-shirt – stared at the enormous turd sprawling in the bowl before him. The fecal brick was gigantic: the tapered end squeezing down the drain, the vast remainder still pretzeled around the inside of the bowl. It had taken the better part of five minutes to push the super shit out of his anus. He had now been staring at it for twice that long, trying to figure out how to get it to flush.

Barry thought about plunging the poop, but there was nothing to plunge. The stool wasn't clogging the drain, it was just too damn big to go down in the first place. He was going to have to break it up into smaller shits.

Barry grabbed the plunger from beside the toilet and sized up the mission before him. The suction cup end wasn't going to help at all. He was going to have to jab it with the wooden end and smoosh his poop into drain-sized chunks. He took a deep breath. Then Barry spun the plunger around. This was not as smooth an action as he had hoped.

As the plunger rotated in his hands, the concave pink end connected with at least three bottles perched behind the toilet: a plastic jug of Drain-Ex, a spray bottle of environmentally-friendly odor remover and the gallon-sized cup of Mountain Dew Sky Blue Crystal (*Now with Real Meth!*[TM]) that Barry had put down when he started pooping.

He watched in horror as all three fell toward the toilet, seemingly in slow motion.

The containers bounced against the seat, the lids all forced open. They bounced again, and again, and then one more time, splashing bleach and sugar water everywhere. The containers spun on the seat edge, and then all three swan-dived into the toilet.

And that's when the explosion happened.

***

Barry Dingle awoke to find himself on his back.

He also really needed to take a shit.

"I *just* pooped," he muttered, reaching absentmindedly for the sink counter with every intention of pulling himself upright. His stomach rumbled.

"Fucking Jack in the Box."

His colon trembled.

"Mother*fucking* Jack in the Box."

As he attempted unsuccessfully to pull himself up, Barry had the vaguest notion that his sink counter was not generally as cold, metal, round and attached to his wrists as it currently felt. He tried to turn and verify this, but his head appeared unable to move, almost as if it were being held stationary by some outside means. This seemed odd. Likewise, Barry, casting his eyes as downward as he could, didn't remember wearing a hospital gown or being strapped to a medical gurney at any point in time prior to his prodigious pooping. Something was clearly up.

"Hello?" he asked. "Anyone here?"

"Oh, good," said a salty voice from just beyond his head, "you're awake."

"It would appear so," replied Barry. "I have several questions regarding that, actually, if you don't mind."

"Not at all."

"OK, first off, how long was I out?"

"It's been three days, six hours and... forty-seven minutes since we found you unconscious in the bathroom. We're not sure how long you were out prior to that."

"OK. OK, good to know... Next question, why am I strapped down? And, on a related note, is this an actual hospital? I'm hearing a lot more screaming than seems normal."

"Excellent questions. You were restrained due to some... disagreement with some of the medications and treatments we used to resuscitate you." Barry heard shuffling and a couple beeps to his left, just out of his peripheral vision. "Your vitals look good now, though, and you seem coherent, so we can probably have the restraints removed shortly."

"And the hospital question?"

"Oh, goodness no. This isn't a hospital."

"Would you care to elaborate on that?"

"I'm afraid I'm not allowed to at this point in time. I'm here in a purely medical capacity; I'm not at liberty to talk about the project itself."

"The project?"

"Medical only," she stonewalled. "Sorry."

"Right, right," said Barry, surprised with himself at how well he was taking things. "One last question, if you don't mind?"

"It's not about the whole 'not a hospital' thing, is it?"

"No."

"OK."

"What," he said remarkably calmly, "in the unholiest of buttfucks happened to me?"

"You don't remember?"

"No," Barry continued, still significantly calmer than he had any right to be, "no, I do not remember what happened. Nothing after my decision to stop at Jack in the Box."

"That was an unfortunate decision, Barry."

"It usually is."

"Well, yeah, OK," said the voice, losing its professional detachment for a moment. "But for more than the usual reasons, I mean. That was a decisively important dinner decision, Barry. Someone will be by soon to explain further."

"How soon is s— You know what? Scratch that.

Priorities are shifting."

Before the voice could ask for an explanation, Barry Dingle's insides answered. His lower intestine gurgled and roared like the Hollywood remake of a B-movie monster.

"Well, this is unexpected," said the salt-throated spokeswoman. There was shuffling and beeping again. "This shouldn't be happening, your bowels should be emptied. All our reports – the numbers, the sheer volume of output –"

"I told you I had Jack in the Box. I had, like, two of those stoner-meal boxes." A wet fart squeaked its way out of Barry's butt cheeks. "Shit. I can't hold this. I'm trying, but… this is happening." A faint trickle of poop juice began running down his thigh. "And God damn soon."

"Right. Uh… fuck," said the voice. "Screw it. Just let it happen, Barry."

A claxon started blaring. A robotic voice trumpeted "Cleaning Team Brown to Lab Seven" over and over again.

"Cleaning Team Brown?"

"This isn't our first rodeo, Barry. We know what we're up against."

Barry's guts turned somersaults. Several sharts begin shooting from his shitter.

"Well, I'm glad somebody does."

"You'll be fine, Barry," said the voice again, presumably trying to be comforting, but mostly raising more questions for the man strapped to the gurney, as it now seemed to be coming from significantly farther away than earlier and muffled by a screen or window of some kind. "Don't fight against your bowels; let what needs to happen, happen."

The smell of burning antiseptic twisted Barry's nose hairs, right up until they fell out completely. His lower intestine began thundering loud enough to drown out the alarms.

"This is gonna suck," he mumbled.

A warm blast of ass gas erupted from his butthole – a prolonged geyser of thick fart – tickling the hair on his balls and pillowing his gown into the air. Ten, then twenty seconds passed, the gaseous shit only compounding, building itself up into a solid state. Thirty seconds. His restraints rattled from the intensity. His asshole felt like it was going to rip in three.

And then Barry Dingle dropped a deuce that blew a hole through the lab's floor.

***

Barry Dingle awoke to find himself once more strapped to a medical gurney in a strange, sterile room. This time, however, he was vertical, and really, really strapped down. He fidgeted against his restraints but wasn't able to move so much as an arm hair. As near as he could tell, his feet were not on the ground.

"Welcome back, Barry," said the salt-voiced woman. "You gave us quite a scare."

Squinting his blurry eyes, Barry was able to make out two figures standing before him. One was clearly the medical technician from earlier. He had no idea who the other one was.

"Where am I? Can you answer that yet?" he asked.

"I can't, no," replied the woman. She appeared to be the figure standing on the left. "As I said I'm strictly here in a medical capacity. However, my colleague here is from –"

"Welcome to Project: Operatives of Psychokinesis, Mr. Dingle," said the tiny man on the right, his voice booming like an empty barrel. "Or, as we like to call it, POP."

"You mean POOP," replied Barry, trying, and failing, to shake his head and speed up the recovery of his vision.

"No, I most certainly do not, Mr. Dingle. We are POP. Your... *abilities* notwithstanding, weaponizing excrement is not a primary –"

"There's two Os. Project: Operatives of Psychokinesis you said, right? That's P-O-O-P. POOP."

"The second O doesn't count, Mr. Dingle."

"Well, yeah, it does. I mean, look, they're not my rules or anything, but, it's POOP. Your organization is POOP."

"No. It's POP. P-O-P."

"You can't discount the second O just because –"

"It's standard APA style, Mr. Dingle. 'Of' isn't capitalized in headings."

"Yes, but a heading is different than an acrostic; you can't drop an entire word just because you don't –"

"Mr. Dingle," the man thundered, "do you honestly think we would have purposely committed this sub-program to the codename Project: Operatives of Psychokinesis if we knew the second O would count?"

"I don't know! I don't know anything about you!" shouted the restrained young man, thrashing ineptly against his tethers. His vision was slowly returning – he could see the deep, rounded corners of the small room; the silver hair and white coat of the medical technician – but the man with the basso profundo voice still appeared to be little more than a smudge in a dark suit.

"Maybe?" Barry added abruptly. "You did seem to be prepared for that shit bomb that exploded out of my butt."

"So you do remember the damage it caused," said the technician, typing feverishly into the tablet she was holding. "This is exce–"

"That was simply because of the evidence provided by previous studies!" bellowed the man. "We've had prior incidents with individuals such as yourself and –"

"So I'm not the first person who could blow stuff up with his dookie?"

"No, you're not," seethed the blurry man in the suit. "But detonative excrement was an accidental discovery of the project, an ancillary and unimportant footnote in our history. Explosive fecal matter is not the program's primary goal! It's not even a tertiary goal!"

"But it is a goal? Somewhere on your list?"

"Recruiting and training field operatives with exploitable psychokinetic abilities is our one and only goal!

The fact that your 'power' is exploding diarrhea is *your* problem, not ours!"

"You're kind of making it POOP's problem, though, aren't you? By keeping me here?"

"IT'S POP, GOD DAMN IT! POP!"

"I'm telling you, you're wrong."

"Why is he still going on about this?" asked the man quietly, turning to the medical technician and shrugging with fury. "Normally there's a lot more crying and threatening to kill us. I actually kind of miss it."

The silver-haired woman rustled through some print-outs and poked and swiped at her tablet a few times, causing a few machines behind Barry to beep.

"Oh, here's the problem," she said. "He's still on some fairly powerful sedatives."

"We should probably stop those then," said the man.

"I'm pretty OK with it," said Barry.

"I'm sure you are." He shook his blurry head and walked out of the room, muttering to himself like Yosemite Sam after a run-in with Bugs Bunny.

"So," said Barry, "how many other folks can poop explosions?"

"More than we'd like," replied the woman, lowering his sedatives from her tablet.

"Give me a percentage."

"At least fifty."

"You're kidding me."

"Unfortunately, no."

"No wonder that tiny, blurry man is so angry about it," said Barry, casting his eyes out the doorway.

"You have no idea," the technician replied, holding her computer against her chest and similarly looking out the doorway after the man in the suit. "He's really bought into the company manifesto. He has all these visions of great things, wonderful things, that we could do to help people if we had the right resources, but all we keep getting are ambitionless slackers that can crap total devastation.

"No offense," she added, turning back to Barry.

"None taken," he replied. Only then did he notice that the woman was no longer a salty voice hovering around a mess of indistinct attributes. She was, quite clearly, an attractive older woman, probably in her sixties, with thick grey hair and eyes like blue diamonds. Her crisp lab coat hung open over a tasteful, and comfortable-looking, pinstriped, slate blue pantsuit that accentuated both her remarkably angular curves and her facial features. Her badge, which, judging by the font and hairstyle, had to be at least twenty years old, said her name was Cyndi L. Klemmerstitch.

She smiled at Barry, revealing only the slightest of wrinkles around the edges of her mouth, and he felt some things of his own wrinkling beneath his gown.

He immediately felt those same things pressing up hard against something he didn't recall being there previously.

As the sedatives and numbness began to fade, the inner parts of his thighs informed him that they, too, were encased in something tight and metal and clearly not meant to be comfortable.

"Am I in some kind of steel underpants?" Barry asked, trying to look down.

"A modified tungsten carbide alloy harness, actually," replied Ms. Klemmerstitch, her smile drifting back to something more professional. "Aside from being another restraint and assisting with the general vertical support of the subject, there is also a suction-powered collection vessel attached to an inclined, cylindrical trough in the rear of the harness in case of another emergency evacuation."

"So, you strapped me into a literal poop chute?"

"Well, I didn't, no. But, yes," she replied with a slight grin, "it's a poop chute. Although, if Mr. von Belgium asks, I most certainly never called it that."

Barry looked again at the man he assumed to be Mr. von Belgium. The man was still pacing back and forth at the far end of the room outside of the room in which Barry was being held, and, presumably, still swearing like a cartoon character. More importantly, though, the man still looked blurry.

The young man in the steel underpants looked at Ms. Klemmerstitch again. She was not blurry. He looked at Mr. von Belgium. His head, and many of his other distinguishing features, looked as if someone had tried to erase them, given up halfway and then broke down sobbing on top of them instead.

"OK, so, what's his deal?" asked Barry, raising an

eyebrow. "Am I still high or is his head a bad Photoshop job?"

"I'm not at liberty to discuss that," said Ms. Klemmerstitch coldly.

"But you see it, right?"

"Yes."

"I'm not hallucinating?"

"No."

"And you're not going to offer anything in the way of explanation?"

"It's not my place."

"What *is* your place?" Barry spat, his patience – and the happy fun time drugs – wearing thin. "And don't say you're 'just medical' again. What the holy hopping hell is going on here? What am I being 'recruited' for, and why has that so far just involved me being tied down?"

"You'll have to ask Mr. von Belgium once he calms down," she said. "Something I suggest *you* do as well."

"Oh my fucking cats." Barry attempted to hang his head in frustration but only succeeded in straining his neck. "Can you at least tell me why my shit makes things explode? That's a medical enough question, right?"

"It is, and we don't know," explained Ms. Klemmerstitch. "That's why you're here, in the med lab. Previous subjects with your… ability have run the gamut from genetic anomalies to a single bad Ethiopian meal with a sewage worker who forgot to wash his hands. There doesn't seem to be a common connection, other than the result. A result POP very much wishes to harness."

"I'm telling you, it should be POOP."

She ignored him and continued: "Until you're able to control your ability – to the satisfaction of both myself and Mr. von Belgium – you'll remain here, in the lab, with the medical team. We're going to work with you to help you govern your powers – control them, contain them, unleash them, use them for the benefit of others. We'll see whether your abilities are relegated strictly to kineto-conductive fecal matter or if there's something less disgusting you can do. Whether it's a physical or mental trigger, physiological, something else. Whether there even *is* a trigger, or whether it's solely containment and damage control at this point.

"To be honest, we don't know for sure yet that the two explosive evacuations thus far are even able to be replicated. All of your numbers, your readings, are giving us nothing to work with, and you yourself seem to have been caught as off guard as we were. This whole thing could very well have been nothing but the Jack in the Box. It wouldn't be the first time."

"So, what I'm hearing," replied Barry, "and correct me if I'm wrong, is that you're holding me here against my will, hoping to learn something that will help you do whatever it is you guys do, something that you can't tell me, by the way, but currently you know nothing about anything and that doesn't appear to be changing anytime soon."

"It can if you can tell us what happened," Ms. Klemmerstitch pleaded. "Why did we found you in your downstairs neighbor's apartment, a hole in his ceiling where your toilet used to be, everything in both your bathrooms, and the one above yours, absolutely saturated with black, watery fecal matter?"

"I have no idea," said Barry. "I didn't even know I had a downstairs neighbor; I thought the place was empty."

"Well, it is now. Poor bastard drowned in your diarrhea."

"You're kidding me."

"I really wish I was," replied the salt-voiced woman, shaking her head. "But I'm not. You murdered an eighty-year-old man with your poop. So maybe you can cut us some slack, OK? We're harboring you, a wanted fugitive, keeping you safe. You think the police will understand this was an accident? Something you couldn't control? Something you don't even remember happening?"

"Probably not, no."

"*Definitely* not, no. You were in the old man's bathroom, on top of his feces-bloated corpse. Your DNA was everywhere, obviously. Not that they'd even need it. What do you think would be easier for the police? To root through three rooms of poop, testing ballistics patterns of runny turds, waiting on blood tests and genetic histories? Or to say you took the idea of a dirty bomb literally, slap you with some goofy label like the Mad Pooper and lock you away forever?

"Tell me, Barry," Ms. Klemmerstitch continued, stepping closer to Barry and putting those dazzling eyes of hers to good use. "What happened that night? How did you convert your bowel movement into a bomb?"

"I honestly don't remember," replied the young man. "I

was super high at the time."

"Think, Barry. We're trying to help you help yourself help us."

He furrowed his brow. "You sure you meant to say that last part out loud?"

"I probably shouldn't have, no."

"Hey, brief change of topic: What, exactly, happens if I don't agree to be 'harnessed' by POOP?"

"It's POP, Barry," she replied, her diamond eyes turning as hard as, well, diamonds. "That's something you can take up with Mr. von Belgium and his associates. Now, is there anything, anything at all, you can tell me about that night? Honestly, at this point I'd settle for any amusing anecdotes involving your digestive system in general."

"Really?" replied Barry, scrunching up his face. "Then you're gonna love this one." He bore down on his guts, squeezing everything he could think to squeeze. Veins throbbed in his neck. He felt something pull in his chest.

"It's not going to work," said Ms. Klemmerstitch dismissively, turning and walking away from Barry Dingle. "The tungsten carbide alloy we use is triple reinforced, made here in one of our –"

Ms. Klemmerstitch had not known this previously, but the sound of three hundred cubic feet of compacted fecal matter violently exploding is best described as *KA-SPLOORMCH*. It was a sound she would never again forget.

The last thing the medical technician saw – lying on her

stomach as she was in a small ocean of shit; half of her face, and most of her back, rubbed and shredded away by the sheer force of the excretory expulsion; and valiantly fighting a losing battle with consciousness – the last thing Cyndi L. Klemmerstitch saw before passing out for the better part of three days was Barry Dingle's ass cheeks shining in the sunlight and dancing in the breeze.

The last thing she heard was Mr. von Belgium bellowing, "Damn it! I knew we should have put these labs underground."

About the Authors

S. N. Atch and S. N. Iff are Siamese twins of differing genders from northern Vietnam, by way of South Korea and the westernmost province of the Philippines. They currently reside in a tiny studio apartment in central Japan, where they operate a Chinese bakery and cafe that specializes in Indonesian pastries and Mongolian beef plates. The twins are originally from a roughshod shack in the heart of the Australian outback, where they were birthed in a tub dirty with dried dingo blood by a Trinidadian midwife to a Panamanian father named Cleveland and a South African mother named Brooklyn. They have a sister named London Virginia who lives in Paris, Texas, with her husband, Dakota Carolina.

Anna "The Ham Ram" Bananarama is heir to the Bananarama fortune. She also co-invented AIDS with Ronald Reagan. The 80s were not her best decade. www.bananarama.co.uk

Ben Dover, Jr. is the son of Ben Dover, the notorious Old West counterfeiter, chicken rustler and all-around asshole. After spending much of his youth moving around, constantly on the run from Johnny Law, Ben Dover, Jr. eventually shot his father in Reno, just to watch him die. Also, to call the cops and get the reward money. He now lives on a very large, very fancy ranch in Colorado with his cat, Ben Dover III, and his ponies, Ben Dovers IV through XVII.

Lavender is the daughter of none of your damn business and watch your fucking mouth. She will fuck you up.

[*Editor's note: Honestly, we're kind of freaked the fuck out by her. Sorry, Lavender. But it's true.*]

Brock A. Lee is always aroused. Always.

H. R. Muffenstoeff is not a pseudonym. Everything she writes is based on her real-life experiences – even, and especially, the shit that doesn't make sense. She is not a compulsive liar, has not dropped a liquid crap into her boss's private coffee maker and does not constantly shave her pubes to the point of irritation because of an irrational fear of crabs. She hopes to one day go to Disneyland, or, alternately, be the first human to fuck a Martian.

Lex Murphy fucking hates dinosaurs.

Billiam Q. Pantoprazole III is your pusherman. Super cool, super clean, he's like an air-conditioned bathroom in the desert that doesn't get used very often: bright, empty and always smelling vaguely of urine.

Johnny Ramrod once rodded a ram so hard his rod rammed right back out the ram's rim and he ended up ramming his rim with his own rod.

Sally Mustang-Leibowitz-Morgan-Jones-Washington-Lee-Redbone, MFA, DDS is a Princess of Hell and the Vice President of Pain and Suffering at their Camden, New

Jersey, office. In her spare time, Mustang-Leibowitz-Morgan-Jones-Washington-Lee-Redbone enjoys sacrificing the souls of the damned, murdering the unborn, kittens, slavery, genocide and kidnapping children. Oh! And rape. Lots of rape. She didn't think she'd be good at it, but it turns out she's got a real talent. At least that's what the federal agents keep saying.

Nathan W. Taynthoemer is the pen name of a rabid jackrabbit whose satchel of fucks-to-give tore a hole and is currently coming up empty.

Do you want an example? I think you want an example.

There was this mime, right, with a baguette in his pants and tied to a telephone pole with an orange extension cord. Nathan saw this and was understandably perplexed. Who would take the time to find a baguette just to stick it in this guy's pants? Exactly how many feet of extension cord does it take to tie up a mime anyway? And what the fuck is a mime doing on the streets of Baltimore in the first place?

So Nathan asked the mime: "Dude, what the hell are you doing?"

The mime began a lengthy charade, hands gesturing everywhere, his eyes glazed over in desperation. As near as Nathan could decipher, the mime had climbed a rope out of an invisible box and nailed himself to a kite. Not seeing a kite or any wounds in the mime's hands. Nathan figured that that was probably wrong and repeated his question. The mime again started to gesticulate frantically, his body writhing against the extension cord. He worked himself into such a frenzy that his eyes began to tear, his veins began to pop and he looked as though he would pass out.

Nathan slapped the mime as hard as he could.

"Speak, damn it! For the love of God, talk, you goofy bastard!"

The mime composed himself as well as a French street performer tied to a telephone phone in Baltimore could be expected to, and apologized for his spastic fit.

"If you could first, please, monsieur, move zee baguette. She is in a very uncomfortable place."

Nathan, with no small trepidation, slid the baked good over a little and the white-faced street performer exhaled deeply.

"Merci."

Then he began his story.

"I was performing here in zee street when I was hastily brushed aside by a large roving black bear and a midget on a unicycle. Zee bear, she was wearing a tutu and running on all fours like someone had yelled 'free croissants,' when suddenly she up-righted herself and threw me bodily into zee storefront over here. She bellowed, she did, at something behind her and ran down zat side street back zere." The mime motioned with his head. "Zee midget, however, he did not make out so well. When zee bear accosted me, zee small one lost his balance and fell off zee unicycle. Zee unicycle then, she fell on top of his tiny frame and he was trapped! I went to help the little man when suddenly I hear a gunshot! Bang! Turning my head, I see a crowd of men dressed in black suits near zee end of zee avenue running toward us. One of zem, he ordered, 'Anozer street performer! Get him!' Not knowing what else to do, I immediately surrender, but still zey feel zee need to kick me in my face. Zee next zing I know, I am blacking out and waking up tied to zees pole."

"So where did the baguette come from?"

"I am not really sure, to be true. But it feels kind of nice now zat you moved it, no? She is kind of soft and like a cushion for my crotch. Feels just like zee bread Mama used to make. But I am digressing. Can you help me down now?"

"Um, no," said Nathan. "No, I can't."

"I'm sorry? You are going to leave me here? Like zees?"

"Yup. Later, Frenchie."

And so Nathan walked away and into the night, wanting nothing more to do with the mime and his fetish for large bread rolls.

He found out the next morning that the mime had died from his wounds. But not the wounds he already had. New ones, added violently and maliciously, by at least six different parties, all coming later that night, after, what was referred to by police as, "a period of time in which the mime probably could have gotten far enough away to not get maimed had he not be tied to a telephone pole by an extension cord."

Nathan felt nothing.

You can email him at taynthoemer@gmail.com or visit taynthoemer.blogspot.com.

Klaus R. Thündercünt was a famous American drunk and exhibitionist who lived during the height of the Revolutionary War. He is best remembered for stealing a horse and riding through the streets of Boston in the middle of the night, pants on his head and ass in the air, screaming incomprehensibly about invading Communists and their death rays and armored zeppelins.

Because Colonial Americans didn't have cable or reliable Wi-Fi and relied mainly on poets to get their news, and also because it was really, really dark out, Thündercünt was incorrectly attributed with creating the first mobile public address system, a contraption built from pots and pans and a complete disregard for the fact that people were trying to sleep, God damn it. While hurriedly trying to file a patent on the invention before William Dawes, another colonial loudmouth, could take proper credit, Thündercünt met office clerk Sarah Orne. The two were married that evening in Niagara Falls, after Sarah's shift ended, flying there in Thündercünt's single engine Cessna and performing the ceremony themselves, in a barrel, as it went over the falls.

Shortly after this famous "Midnight Bride," Klaus R. Thündercünt put down the better part of a quart of whiskey, fell into a pond and was frozen into a six-foot-tall ice cube. Found almost two hundred years later by the Incredible Hulk, Thündercünt joined the Avengers, got a naïve teenager killed, punched Hitler in the face and then won the Vietnam War with nothing but his dashing good looks and a borrowed spoon. He retired from crime-fighting soon thereafter, moving to a nice place in the country and founding an orphanage in Buenos Aires for heroin-addicted kittens.

Sadly, Thündercünt was assassinated by a Skrull sniper just days after the ground-breaking. He was thirty-five years old.

His email is <u>thoonderkoont@gmail.com</u> and is maintained weekly by his ghost.

Catherine Uncer Napolitano Tijeras is just the worst bitch you've ever met. She also has three of the nastiest pussies known to mankind. Constantly scratching up her couch and shitting in her Cheerios. Her vagina's also pretty nasty. Shit has lasers. Enter at your own risk. And don't even THINK about going 'round back. Her a-hole will bite your dick off. Literally. She suffers from an affliction called anal dentata and there is currently no known cure.

Helga Louise Tikkelfitz lost her vagina in the war. The Class War. She has since given birth to three beautiful baby boys. Through her butt.

SHE'S A WITCH! BURN HER!

No, guys, it was science, not –

BUUUURRRRNNN HEEEERRRRR!!!